*say this*

ALSO BY ELISE LEVINE

*This Wicked Tongue*
*Blue Field*
*Requests and Dedications*
*Driving Men Mad*

ELISE LEVINE

# SAY

*two novellas*

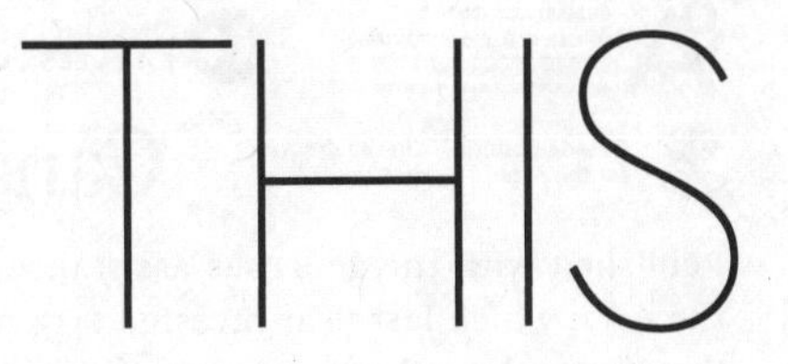


A JOHN METCALF BOOK

BIBLIOASIS
*Windsor, Ontario*

FIRST EDITION

10 9 8 7 6 5 4 3 2 1

Library and Archives Canada Cataloguing in Publication
Title: Say this : two novellas / Elise Levine.
Names: Levine, Elise, author.
Identifiers: Canadiana (print) 20210293470
Canadiana (ebook) 20210293489
ISBN 9781771964609 (softcover)
ISBN 9781771964616 (ebook)
Classification: LCC PS8573.E9647 S29 2022 | DDC C813/.54—DC23

Edited by John Metcalf
Copyedited by Emily Donaldson
Text and cover designed by Natalie Olsen

Published with the generous assistance of the Canada Council for the Arts, which last year invested $153 million to bring the arts to Canadians throughout the country, and the financial support of the Government of Canada. Biblioasis also acknowledges the support of the Ontario Arts Council (OAC), an agency of the Government of Ontario, which last year funded 1,709 individual artists and 1,078 organizations in 204 communities across Ontario, for a total of $52.1 million, and the contribution of the Government of Ontario through the Ontario Book Publishing Tax Credit and Ontario Creates.

PRINTED AND BOUND IN CANADA

*For John Metcalf*

*Vid Smooke*

If you could talk what would you say?

SLEATER-KINNEY
*One More Hour*

Is not everything the search?

JOY WILLIAMS
*Bromeliads*

*contents*

# EVA HURRIES HOME

SON ONE

# I

# *everything has already happened*

The fog and its clearing. The fog again, a clouded mirror.
Eva's cousin. His slender back.

Eva's cousin, his slender back. She washes it twice. The first time, the bathroom steams. She applies the worn terrycloth to the mole near the base of his spine, as best she can make out. Just above his crack. She drips water along his neck. Exactly as his dead sister did. The knobs along his spine flex as he speaks. Eva stops. She hadn't known about a dead sister. Exactly the same. Eva dips the cloth again into the tub. She strokes his forearms and chest. Am I hurting you? Rain hisses against the roof. Eva's cousin falls asleep in the cooling water while she crouches on her heels. His long lashes, full lips. Sort-of moustache. The rain stops. A car crunches on the gravel drive. A car door slams. Eva closes the bathroom door behind her.

Sixteen would be right—when on a cloud-jammed July afternoon her cousin sweeps aside his curtain of long hair, leans across the kitchen table and plants a swift kiss. He is twenty-one. He still lives in this old house on a hill with his stepmother who works and works. His nose upturns to a point. He is slight, not tall. It's the house that is tall, and taller that afternoon in the kitchen. The ceiling shoves up and the air thins and Eva and her cousin grow tiny, turn into small, amazing children. His laugh foams. Outside the kitchen window, the steeply serried streets of Astoria, Oregon. Whitecaps curl on the river below town. Freighters and distant forests bear crowns of mist. If she's sixteen, it's 1993. Let's go for a drive.

She's sixteen, sure. The songs he'll write about her when he gets famous, providing he can sweet-talk his stepmother into buying that red guitar. His collection of seven silver dollars he'll split with Eva once their value jacks. Loopy grin each time he takes his gaze from the wet road. Clogs her throat so hard it's like dying except probably better. It's raining hard when he turns onto an old logging road and the car shudders into the woods. Trees splash above. He brakes and turns off the engine. Smokes, pops the top on a brew. The windows glaze. The air grows thick. He hikes her thin skirt and lifts the band on the leg of her underwear with an inquisitive finger and hunches over her. Spilled beer pools on the floor mat. His cat tongue makes sticky sounds. So much rain. Eva comes hard. Really hard. He kisses her bare, beer-sticky soles. He rubs himself on her, all over her. He gentles her head down.

After, Eva's cousin sits propped in the tub like a pale boy-king tired from a long day of chasing puppies and tying ribbons in girls' hair and chewing meat soaked in milk.

The white-flower cups of his knees. The bathroom window wide open, a fat moon. Eva covers her cousin's face with the ratty washcloth. As if admiring her handiwork, she takes in his narrow chest, the delicate neck. Slick with water, his thatch of brown hair resembles the fur of a sleek animal that changes with ease. She wonders if she can. Is she already? In a strangled voice he says, Still like me?

Do you? Eva thinks, though not often, over the course of the next twenty-five years. Or twenty-eight. Or twenty-seven. She can never be sure. Her mind glazes. She only knows the affair was their last summer together, before she flew back east for the final time. Left for good. Still like me? Miss me. Think of me.

# II

## *commute*

Eva is at work when she gets the email. It's 2018, a cold spring. A famous journalist wants to know, can he talk to her? He lists his main credentials, but she mostly already knows who he is and the rest she quickly googles.

Twenty-five years ago, possibly around the time of Eva's affair with her cousin, the journalist published a book on basketball as played by teens in a small town in North Carolina. The book became the basis for a movie and a TV series. Since then he has written about his designer-clothing obsession and how he hates fucking his second wife. He has written a respectful, thoughtfully inflected as-told-to with a transgender reality-TV star.

In the email the journalist is professional and polite. He's in the research stage for a book he's writing under contract. It's about Eva's cousin. Can she help?

Eva hits *reply*. She stares at the empty space where her standard demurral will go. She is no stranger to such requests, though they had dwindled to nothing as time wore on, as hopefuls checking family connections failed to turn up fruitful leads.

She rereads the journalist's words. He lives in southern Washington State, not far from Astoria, Oregon, in the same coastal region her cousin once had. This is the reason, in part, for the journalist's abiding interest. It haunted him all the while he was tied to other projects, unable to get the story out of his head. He has tracked her down through her cousin's stepmother, who gave Eva's name. It took the journalist a while to figure it out, but he's pretty sure she's the right person. Can she confirm?

Eva is late for her afternoon meeting. She closes her laptop and pushes from her desk. She stands. Her breath clicks in her throat.

The old woman is still alive. News to Eva. She never received a response to the several letters she wrote, and the last time she checked, she can't remember how long ago, the phone number was unlisted.

Eva tucks her laptop under her arm. She straightens her shirt collar around her suit jacket and gathers her keys and ID on their lanyard.

She is halfway to the elevator bank when she realizes she pressed *send* on the blank.

Early evening. Washington, DC. Eva at forty-one. She sweeps through the downpour. Gutters choke and traffic stands still. Chins bob beneath black umbrellas. Her bare legs are chilled raw. She has trains to catch. She has terrible thoughts. Tears were shed at the afternoon meeting but not by her—not yet. The world at large also continues to exist—for now. No lunatic has yet pushed a button. Colossal fires and floods and migratory cataclysms rage elsewhere, but for now she and her world are safe.

Only the smell of damp bodies rises from the Dupont Metro entrance. Belowground she swipes her card at precisely the same moment as a stranger on her left and a stranger on her right. The turnstiles clatter open and Eva and her shadows charge through. The gates clank shut behind and, in a burst of self-consciousness or misplaced competitive spirit or an untethered fear, difficult sometimes to distinguish among them, Eva breaks ranks and bolts.

Another floor down, a worker on the opposite platform sponges a section of tiled wall where graffiti lunges in magenta. GIVE ME HEAD TILL I'M DEAD. Eva's train roars in and she shoulders aboard.

She gets off at Union Station and locates her track for the MARC, hurries and attains an aisle seat beside an older woman playing a game on her phone. Thin humanoid shapes spindle outside a tall clapboard house on a hill. Twilight. The woman taps the screen. A very old woman appears at the house's front door. Another tap and a grinning ginger saunters across the porch, sits and licks its paw.

The train rumbles from the station and Eva fishes a book from her bag and tries to read. It's snowing in Norway. A fox slips through drifts. A woman lingers beneath a streetlight, some crime to solve.

Eva can't quite follow. She closes the book on her lap. Across the aisle a man eats a succession of breath mints from a tin. Cleaning-solvent smell. The woman next to Eva rests her wet sleeve against Eva's and falls asleep.

Eva cannot sleep. Before she left the office, she read the journalist's second email, apparently sent in reply to Eva's accidental non-response. He expects she has insights. That she more than draws blanks. In sharing what she knows, she might help others to heal. For example, the family of the victim, who despite the thirteen years that have passed since the murder and the two years of trial hell continue to suffer the after effects. For example, the close friends and associates, and those the victim served over the years in his capacity as respected lawyer, champion of the underdog—these people continue to endure emotional burdens too. Despite the eleven years since Eva's cousin began serving his sentence in a federal penitentiary in Oregon. There is still, there must be, the possibility to mend.

For Eva too, the journalist bets. He would like to know, how has she felt, what does she think, how have the murder and sentencing and serving changed her? Surely they have?

Aggravated murder, the journalist noted toward the end of this email. Her cousin lucky. Instead of the death penalty that Oregon still had at the time, he got life with no parole. His sentence the result of a deal he struck for his cooperation, which allowed the authorities to locate and recover the victim's body. Quite the story, the journalist said.

Eva could almost hear his appreciative whistle.

The train trundles over the tracks and she rocks from side to side. Why tell her what she already knows? He strikes her as presumptuous, vaguely threatening. As if he believes he holds some kind of power over her. As if she's in no position to refuse to cooperate.

Prick. His aggressive bullshit the same as those who preceded him. The assertion that he's different from the rest who might have, who surely have, contacted her. The declaration that he alone wants to understand the case at granular and global levels. Will strive to unpack the legal and psychological ramifications, uncover the nuances. Get into the weeds and soar above, see a humanizing justice done for all.

Including Eva. He has set his heart on it. Wouldn't talking to him help her too? He expects it might.

Wants, expects. Eva flushes cold. Is this guy for fucking real?

Outside the train window, platforms and commuter parking lots bubble with black water. Between stations, darkness scrawls.

The conductor announces Odenton next and Eva's head jerks. She swipes drool from the corner of her mouth. The woman next to Eva grapples upright and she swings her legs sideways to let the woman shuffle past. Her yellowing hair brushes Eva's cheek and she tries not to recoil.

The main lights flicker and go out. The car goes silent. Now what? the woman huffs, a dim bulk in the aisle. She peers accusingly at Eva through thick lenses that seem coated with a greasy film.

She shrugs and reopens her book, flips pages, though it's hard to see the words clearly now.

After a minute the engine roars. The main lights switch on again and Eva's seatmate is gone, the man across the aisle vanished.

The train lumbers forward. Sodden trees and shrubs, tentatively leafed, black the sky. Up an incline, a deer wavers in the rain.

Past BWI Eva stows her book in her bag and collects her dripping umbrella from between her feet, but the train idles outside the West Baltimore station, last stop before hers. No explanation for the wait is announced over the intercom but Eva suspects flooding. Expects. The waters rise often in Baltimore streets and basements, though not her own basement or street. She lives on a modest-sized hill where there is good drainage, a consideration she took into account when she bought the place two years ago—and anyway the previous owner thoughtfully, neurotically installed a sump pump next to the washer-dryer. Eva does sometimes notice seepage and mould blooms. Par for the course in the city's ruinous humidity, but nothing like the catastrophes she sometimes reads about in the news. Sinkholes that crack open to swallow sidewalks and cars. Occasionally someone hurt or killed.

She leans back again in her seat.

Here are her own knees, knobby and chapped. Her middle-aged face shorn of detail in the vaporing window.

The train jolts to life again. The shitty weather continues.

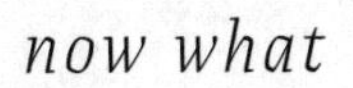

# III

*now what*

The shuttle bounces north on Charles Street. Shops are closing, closed, the sidewalks deserted. The Wyman Park Dell like a blank pool. The art museum puts in a luminous appearance, flood-lit exterior ascendant above the park's massed treetops, the neon sculpture near its rooftop flashing VIOLENCE VIOLINS SILENCE VIOLINS VIOLENCE SILENCE.

Eva misses her stop. She gets off and doubles back. The university's winding red-brick pathways seem empty but for horizontal slashes of rain. She clutches her useless umbrella and leans into the wind, lamppost to lamppost to blue security post. Her teeth chatter. The marble facings on retainer walls shiver with rivulets. Near the glass pavilion, two students skip by, jackets hoisted over their heads, laughing like gulls.

Eva spies the clock tower and nears the library with its marble dome and books moled away in the basement levels like material for pervs. Not that she's been inside. She has only heard rumours based on insider-knowledge she herself does not possess, though she works for this very university—but as staff and not faculty, and at another division. She's a number cruncher, name-taker, maker of lists at the satellite campus in the capitol, where she cannot afford to live.

At least she still has her job. For now. Two months ago her division announced a convulsion of restructuring moves. A kill-off among staff. Contracts that will not be renewed come June, the end of the fiscal year.

Eva climbs the steps to the library anyway, attracted by the radiance of a gathering in the rotunda, visible through the plate glass. A large cake with white icing edged in coral on a long table draped in a white tablecloth. A young woman with short orange hair and pale oval face who stands at the centre of the crowd. She opens and closes her mouth like a pretty fish.

Eva opens and closes her own mouth and the cold skittles through her on its way elsewhere. The young woman gives a faint curtsy to a froth of clapping hands, and Eva bows her bedraggled head and dips too. Her heart leaps then drops. Shame on you, Eva. Exhibit A at the trial of How Low Have You Gone? Living or pretending to live another person's life—not for the first time.

The crowd inside readies to leave. Doors open and close. Water blows in sheets down the marble stairs and Eva melts back into the storm.

Almost home, jiggety-jig. Lightning flashes on bewilderments of daffodils. Windows glow and porch lights burn to deter crime on this nice-enough block of smallish row homes built in the 1920s. Things could be worse. Eva crosses the street to avoid a tree branch sprawled across the sidewalk. She steps around a manhole cover, known to pop in heavy rains. She reaches the curb and the wind gusts, her umbrella turns inside out. Another gust and her hair swims into the air and tentacles around her head.

A workplace farewell for Eva? Not on her life. She minds her own business, and too many of her co-workers have recently gone, unsung, before her.

Coming to the end—then what? Blank space. Vertigo. Would it be so bad? Before the anxiety of having to find another job kicked in. Static. No slow fade and zoom out. Instead a fast black. A twist and something else tuning in.

Some song stuck in her head.

Her cousin in her head. He's facedown on the beach, not far from the waterline, sleeping or pretending to. Dark sand sugars the backs of his thighs. A stiff breeze raises goosebumps along his torso and arms. A radio bleats beside him. Waves kick their fuss closer on the incoming tide. Not much farther up the shore, a rotting seal rocks half in, half out of the water. Soon the body will soak out to sea.

Eva stands on her porch, rucking in her tote for her front-door keys. A cry and a leap and the neighbour's tabby rubs its wet fur on Eva's calves. Hello, my pretty! What big stripes you have.

Eva resumes her search and locates her keys. Her phone too. The screen is broken. No idea when or how that happened. The thought of the cost and hassle involved in replacing the device makes her feel like lying down in the middle of the street for a month or six.

Out of habit, she taps the shatter pattern to unlock it and discovers the thing still works.

Bar? Kara's text says between the cracks. Reza's text says he craves Thai.

Eva jams open the front door—it sticks in the humidity. As usual, the thought of fixing it exhausts her. She hangs her coat on the inner-door handle, removes her boots and lays her umbrella open on the entryway rug. Her ankles ache. She craves only a glass of water. The motions of drawing a bath and brushing her hair. Lying back in the tub.

There now. The strangeness of toes. Of metallic-blue nail polish. Her bathroom window streams.

In the bedroom Eva pulls on a sweater and jeans. Made it, still here, in one piece. She thinks. Still here the mid-week and the world that contains it. Or at least rattles nearby, like the window, which faces the rain-muffled street.

The room is stuffy. A spackle of black mould decorates the flanges on the ductless AC/heat unit above the bed. She should disinfect, clean the whole place. This Sunday or the next. She should wear a mask in here. Or something.

She turns off the overhead light and ditches her clothes. It is bad. Only Wednesday, so very Wednesday. She curls onto the bed and props the phone against her chest. The storm renews itself with thunder, lightning. Eva does not renew herself. She should eat. Get up, go out. Somewhere beery and clammy with a packed-in crowd. The Dizz or the place on 29th. She should do something. Want something. At the very least, thumbs-up her friends' texts and offer apologies. Read about a fox in snow, some crime. Entertain more thoughts and not lie here, a Miss Fill-in-the-Blank. Like that is her job title or something.

Or continue to lie here, if she feels like it.

She feels like it.

Another message buzzes her heart. Do not resuscitate, she back-talks the text.

Another song in her head.

Her cousin again in her head. Wind and waves, a grey west coast. Rain like a scrim against which anything is possible. Grainy projections of his cock in her hand. Her mouth. Something inside her curious as fingers probing her cunt.

What was she even, back then? Sixteen, fifteen. Thirteen—could she have been that young?

Remember me, think of me. Miss me.

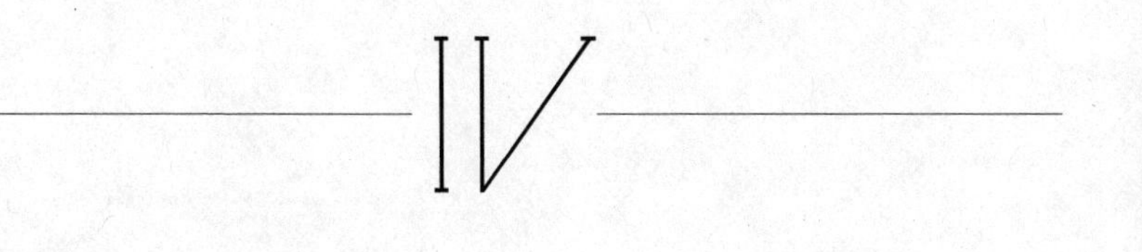

# IV

*departures*

At nine-thirty the next morning Eva is at work tending her to-do lists. One on a series of large blue Post-its. One on a pad of lined paper. Another for her pocket-sized spiral-bound notebook.

A third email from the journalist arrives. It rattles and surprises her. For god's sake, it's six-thirty in the morning his time.

Please, he says in the first paragraph, the first paragraph in its entirety.

His second paragraph, in full: Can I count on you?

His third and final paragraph is a sign off: Are you my little bird?

Dear god. Is this worm actually flirting with her?

Eva's boss crinkles her face. Bruised-looking pouches rim her sockets. Her eyes water. She pulls a tissue from her purse and dabs them.

With these numbers, she says, scratching and digging at her scalp, I'm not sure we'll make it. The numbers don't lie.

Eva and her boss, Tina, are seated at a table in the Bunting Institute's cafeteria, two buildings from the university's DC digs, where Tina is the registrar and Eva is the assistant registrar for the university's non-traditional learners division. These Thursday lunches are usually a highlight of the week for Eva. She lives it up, prowling the elaborate salad bar bedecked with potted hyacinths in spring, poinsettias in winter, plasticky looking gourds in fall, acquiring her roasted Brussels sprouts and jicama-carrot medley while rubbing shoulders with the sharply dressed multilinguals who staff the Institute. Sleeksters who make Eva feel mildly aspirational, as if she had a weak case of the flu.

Today the rain is still driving down and the cafeteria is super-muggy and super-under-inspiring. She noticed a few people in the cashier lines wearing surgical masks, ill or afraid of illness. Eva herself feels brain-fuzzy and slightly nauseous, as if she too is getting sick or afraid of getting sick.

Also, what Tina says is true. The numbers do not lie.

Enrollments continue to death spiral, as they have all year. The projections are screwed. It's the boom-bust from global economic disparities. Infectious waves of uncertainty over climate shifts and habitat destruction, potential pandemics. A hateful federal administration. The university administration's mandate to not give a shit about anything other than the paucity of butts in seats. The mandate to severely curtail, for the sake of maintaining division profitability, rather than shore up long-debilitated infrastructure and improve academics to make them more competitive. The mandate to hollow out, pillage, destroy.

Ergo the staff cull.

More heads will roll, Tina whispers, raking her fingers through her dark hair. Her nose shines. Her ultramarine power pantsuit is rain-spotted and rumpled, as was yesterday's red pantsuit—the state of her suits alone is enough to make Eva lose hope. Add in Tina having to cancel her usual quarterly session at the leadership conference in Albuquerque next week and the situation appears truly dire. Though she does maintain her promise to again tirelessly advocate for Eva's yearly COLA raise when the annual reviews and contract renewals come up.

If Eva's even come up. She nods morosely and swallows an olive slice. Chief of Data Analysis, gone. Pre-contract-renewal season! Courtesy of the legal loopholes everyone signed for on the dotted line. Assistant Director of Admissions, gone. Two assistant marketing specialists, nearly done for, according to the rumour mill.

But THE MANDATE. The situation is an EMERGENCY. The Deans are freaking. The Deans are asking, pointedly, eyebrows arched, squinting eyes gone squintier. HOW, they roar, slapping palms on conference tables, HOW can the division up-leverage its brand? Increase their offerings of stackable learnables? Convince more potential learner-consumers to shift their career lattices? People, COME ON. Only INNOVATIVE thinking permitted here.

Eva nudges a clump of kale with her fork. Tina scratches and some of her hair floats into her tilapia with lemon sauce, today's special. Red welts score the white patches between her brunette clumps. These days there is a permanent sweat-line like a mustache on her upper lip that Eva can barely restrain herself from wiping away. She can hardly keep from spitting nails and screaming at her boss's bosses, Assistant Dean Muckity and Associate Dean Muck, during the endless EMERGENCY meetings. She's hardly even trying to keep her poorly paid job.

Which at least is a job, dumb though it is. She must keep that in mind.

But talk about dumb. When was the last time she herself learned anything? When her own mind sparked and leapt? When she didn't feel dead inside from taking calls to commiserate with adult students needing to drop their classes because they've lost their jobs and need a full tuition refund. Eva on the phone day in and day out explaining division policy. Explaining no exceptions. Explaining out of luck. Eva crushed inside, herself potentially job-insecure, disposable.

She forces herself to chew. She can innovate. Magic shit up. Her best brainchild involves her and Tina and Tina's young daughter, who closely resembles her mom, judging by the framed pictures on Tina's desk. In Eva's big plan they abscond to a dreamy lair on a secret island, along with Tina's mother, a recent immigrant from the Philippines, who cares for the child while Tina is at work.

Eva sips her glass of tap water. Yes, Grandma too. Eva never knew her own grandparents and so is able to idealize such entities, she admits it. Yes, this old woman will embrace them all in her generous and soothing old arms.

Tina sighs. Yes, she says, agreeing with herself. More heads will certainly roll. Let's hope they're not our own.

Out of appreciation for Tina's use of the first-person plural, Eva manufactures a gasp and opens her eyes wide. Though she is already way past her boss on the possibility of being let go—she gives herself two months tops.

You think? Eva says.

Tina wiggles her shoulders and kneads her neck. Who's to say? she says.

It's devastating to see Tina so low. Until recently, she's been one of three experienced and competent employees of colour working higher-up admin jobs in the division. The other two having recently been canned, Tina might well also find herself done for and replaced. Possibly by a lower-salaried person of colour.

But if our heads roll, Eva offers, we might never find them!

Clumsy, Eva. As is her deserted island fantasy. Just entertaining it smacks of white saviourism, right? Clumsy and far, far worse.

But Tina laughs at Eva's silly remark—Tina a generous, beautiful spirit. She also possesses great teeth, which remain in evidence seconds later when she trains them on the assistant finance specialist, who cringes past the table clutching a non-recyclable take-out container. Tina reaches out a hand and waves—beautiful! Eva's own eyes water.

I feel badly for her, Tina says when the specialist is out of earshot. It must be lonely in that head.

Eva pictures the sad, cubicle-girded desk lunches. At the washroom sinks, glances averted from the tearful just-fired.

At least we still have each other, Tina says.

We do! Eva chirps. Right? It's not so bad!

Tina's face seems about to dissolve like paper in the rain, then her expression hardens.

Stupid, Eva. It is bad. Tina is mother to a young child, Tina brought her elderly mother over, Tina is sole breadwinner in this heartbreaking fuckwad economy.

Eva bites the inside of her cheek to keep herself from liquefying. To keep holding on. She hopes it doesn't show.

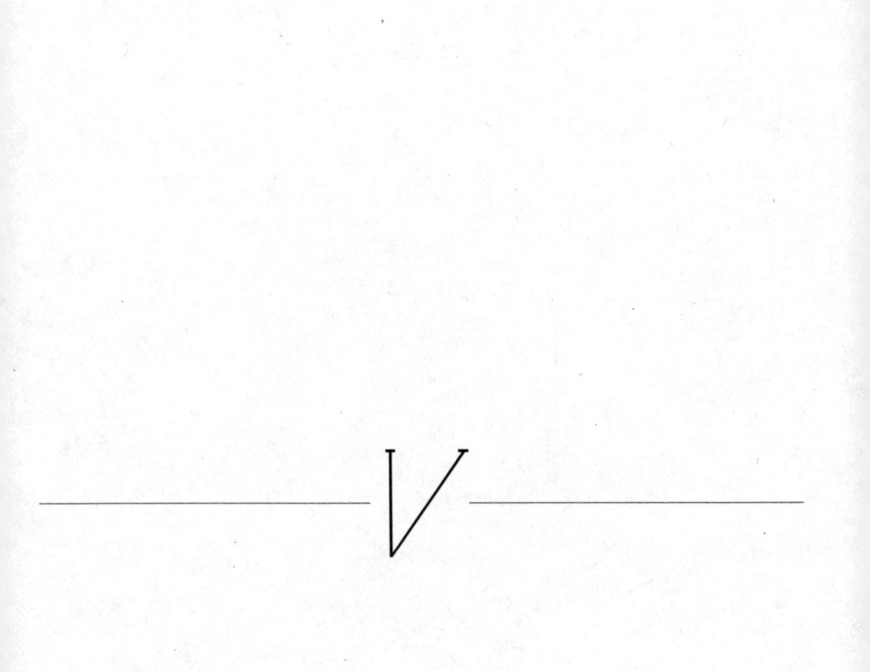


# *nothing she likes*

Night again. Eva is once more on her porch, soaked and searching for her keys. She crouches and dumps the contents of her bag. Did she not used to have her shit together? When did the shift happen? When she learned her job might vaporize? She grubs her hands among her stuff.

A quick movement beside her and the neighbour's tabby foxes his damp fur against Eva's haunches, her vision trembles, a fast black and then the sky brightens in a flash.

Waves pound the shore. She lifts the band on the back of her cousin's trunks and runs a finger along his tan line. He doesn't move. She wonders if he's asleep. Is she?

Not asleep. It is early evening and the cat bats Eva's shin and sticks its claws in her pant leg, grazing the skin. Beat it, she yawps, bolting upright, trying to break free. Scram-ola.

Mee-oww, says sleepy cousin.

The sand beneath him is blinding. His right arm swings fast and he grasps Eva's wrist. Hurts. He rolls onto his hip and displays the shadowed erection tenting his trunks.

Eva hunches over, slides her hands between her thighs and presses. She remembers to breathe, unhooks the animal from her pants and toes it onto the wet porch steps. There—she's good, no worries. It's good to have prised away at least one stuck thing.

She scoops up the contents of her tote and after three tries shoves her front door open. And another thing: she will scrape enough together or take on debt to hire someone to fix the fucking door. While she still has her fucking job. Getting her front door fixed: that's something she can do. Will do.

She hangs up her coat, lays her boots beside her umbrella on the entryway rug. Done and done and what next? Something important has slipped her mind. Air fevers her forehead. The thermostat schedule must be off, the heat on all day. Or she really is coming down with something. A furball drifts along the hallway floor, though she has never owned a cat.

Suck, her cousin says, the word squeezed out beneath his sort-of stache.

He tightens his grip. His eyes form slits.

You, he says. Suck.

Hot crush. Got her good.

# VI

*Eva orders in*

Jiggety-jig, still Thursday night. Eva is on her couch. She picks at her take-out, sickened to admit it: she is attracted by the journalist's celebrity and rep. Impressed, flattered. Tempted: guilty as charged.

His promise that she matters, that her contribution to the story of her cousin can make some kind of difference, are the same lures she has dodged the past eleven years, ever since she learned of the murder he committed two years prior. Promise that her cousin's story will give form to her feelings. Promise of containment, if not outright eradication.

She again goes through the reasons for her distrust.

Her parents shipping her, their sole child, west each summer to give themselves together-alone time.

Her lonely-girl affair with her much-older cousin when she was how old.

Years later, the murder. In its wake, a shiver of hucksters on the scent of a salacious story, chum for vicarious, titillating blood sport. How could she be sure she wouldn't be contributing?

Her answer is still no. She will email the journalist tomorrow.

She has her chosen other life. Which does not involve sorting out what happened between her and her cousin or reckoning with the fact of the murder and what she might or might not feel about it. She is all about home to work to home. Drinks or dinner with friends. A few relationships that felt serious at the time but which she is relieved have ended, the most recent two years ago. She is relieved at the lack of demands. She is not lonely. Bored with work, sure. Stressed now with the specter of its potential disappearance. But happy to be on her own, herself by herself, free.

Absolutely—if not for the recent bullshit meltdown of her job, she'd be happy AF. Mindlessly content inhabiting a usefully boring tale like the kind displayed in museum cases, cuneiform incised on clay tablets, the earliest and remarkably dull written accounts. Lists and tallies not so different from her own daily to-dos. What adds up. Three jugs of wine, six of oil, two goats.

Job she might soon lose. She might slip into another other life. A new job title: Someone Who Does Not Amount to Much. A Person Who Does Not Add Up.

She drops her chopsticks into a food container and covers her face with her hands. This journalist has caught her at a shaky moment. She's a soft target, as she once was for her cousin, when she was a lonely girl shipped nearly a continent away each summer by her parents, who claimed to need their own headspace, apart from her.

She does remember. She does think about him. She admits it, guilty as charged.

She bundles into two sweaters and fixes a drink, sits on her porch in the dark and listens to the rain. The neighbour's tabby curls at her feet as if it owns her.

Cats—Eva flicks her shoulders. Her cousin's stepmother had a cat and little else. Just her cleaning jobs and her falling-down house on a hill. Peeling paint. Loose floorboards. Smell of salt and mould.

And Eva's cousin to raise on her own ever since his father, the old woman's husband, got himself thrown in the slammer. For something Eva can't remember. He was the only brother of her mother, their connection but a tenuous thread.

Eva bitched to her cousin once about the mustiness, which also permeated the streets.

Better here than Portland, Eva's cousin told her with a cool feline smile. Portland smells like piss.

Two more drinks in and Eva remembers her cousin's smiles as strange beasts. Distinct from the unhinged grin reserved for seductions and raw sex. One smile a cold twitch of delicate cheeks. Another a buzzy haze in his eyes. Like the fireflies he trapped on warm nights. Roaming the uncut lawn, he'd cup the insects one by one in his palms, make a glowing cage of his fingers, tip them into a row of jars nestled in the weeds.

When she was twelve or fourteen, or what. Pre-sex? So much time has passed, blurred time, and now the exact numbers float on a blank screen behind her eyes much as the fireflies floated against the dark.

What do you think they're saying? Eva's cousin asked one night.

All down the line, fireflies lit and spent themselves and Eva's skin tingled as if they'd crawled inside her. How could she say that?

Nothing? Miss Blanky?

He stood close to her and put the flat of his hand on the small of her back. He rubbed slow circles and heat laddered from her crotch up her spine. A glimmer of an idea crawled inside her ear and tickled. She couldn't for the life of her trick it forward into her mind and bend words to serve it.

He stretched his arms high and yawned and she smelled his sharp sweat. He dropped his hand on top of her head and waggled it. Bobble bobble.

If Eva did as he said, maybe he'd clue her in.

If Eva crept down the stairs to the kitchen in the middle of the night while the old bitch slept, and poured him a glass of milk.

If Eva sounded the alarm when the old cow's station wagon pulled into the drive on afternoons when he read his magazines on the couch, a wad of toilet paper at the ready beside him.

If Eva washed his back when he sat in the tub while the old cunt scrubbed the grander houses in town, or up the peninsula in Washington State where rich people built handsome bayside homes with perfect views and drove out the oystermen, but what can you do?

Not that Eva's cousin did much in terms of work. Or seemed to want to. He grumbled about the changing local economy, a disastrous shift away from the cannery and once-plentiful longshoremen jobs, but his complaints just seemed like things for him to say. His stepmother bleached and vacuumed herself ragged across town and the bridge that crossed the state line and the lower Columbia River, cleaned her way north along the Long Beach Peninsula while he lounged. In that rambling house and on Astoria's rougher streets. Through the stench of their alleys and on the local roads and highways in his shit-box Tercel. Alone and seemingly friendless except for Eva during her summer visits, when her squabbling parents shipped her west from Jersey.

This was after his mother died in the car crash. It was after his father, Eva's mother's brother, remarried and got sent to prison for something Eva was never able to figure out—her mind veiled by years of her own parents, their eternal-seeming splitting or getting back together before they finally divorced, those years of declaring themselves not up to dealing with anyone but themselves.

Visiting her cousin, abandoned to his own devices by an absent father and a stepmother working herself to death, Eva discovered her own space. In that house on a hill with its under-furnished and lopsided rooms opening one into another like pieces of a puzzle. On the splintery porch where she perfected her slouch and surveyed the river, gathering thunderheads, the distant bark and bellow of the sea lions that congregated around the town's docks. Along the coastline's sandy largesse, where she learned from her cousin to smoke fat spliffs beside rip-tide waters. Thick garlands of clouds overhung them and sometimes a jolt of blue sky like the inside of blown glass.

Or atilt down Astoria's steep streets toward the liquor store with her cousin, zipping past the alley men while he traded insults with them. Work of sorts when he wasn't dealing weed, clearing dead tree branches or removing expired raccoons from attics for small change.

His job—to take care of her. The girl who loved him. His small, sad cousin who for a handful of summers had nowhere else to go. The pair of them two lost souls.

A third smile. Like his first, frigid as mid-winter. A corner of mouth upturned. His face a locked treasure chest stored at the bottom of an ice-bristled creek. A place she might have come upon in a quest to figure shit out. Had the desire struck.

Down among the water weeds and soggy trash. To get there, her pockets stuffed with stones.

Or it is more like he was inside her like rocks. Heavy and sharp. Still is. Can't get him out.

Fuck the journalist. As if she needs him to remind her. She stomps inside and hauls her laptop from the coffee table. For fuck's sake, she can check the bookmarked page herself.

Her cousin at the arraignment. Thirteen years ago. Two years before Eva found out about it. His image splashed on the pages of any number of west coast newspapers at the time. He is erect, narrow chest puffed inside the orange jumpsuit. Hands cuffed in front. Head held high. No sort-of moustache, but a smile she does not recognize. Lips curled faintly upward and covering his teeth as if he were amused by a private joke. Not a smile—a smirk. An actual fucking smirk.

His skin is a meth hound's. Picked raw. His teeth possibly black stumps.

It is beyond thinking: her love for her cousin once upon a time.

She studied this photo over and over when she first learned about the murder, and finally declared a moratorium. A ban on sleepless nights and rot-wracked sleep. Shaking limbs, plunging moods. Thinking and thinking, sifting through the past for clues. About him, herself, especially herself. Had she in some way been complicit, not sounded some alarm? Guilty, not guilty. On the hook, off. Fights picked with Lena, Eva's longest-term romantic partner, over nothing. Lena's tears and later her hard resolve, asking Eva to leave the townhouse in Silver Spring. That panicked feeling again, from childhood. Feeling of the shunted off, the housing insecure. For where on earth would Eva go? What place might hold her? A pity party, since she managed, of course. Rented her own place and ceased and desisted looking up her cousin's trial. Dated other people. Stopped dating, got serious and bought this house. The ban held.

Obvious—her looking and thinking had done no one, herself included, any good. Obvious she should stop for good. That she could, and she did. Let herself off the hook.

The pang shoots out of nowhere: he never did like showing his crooked teeth.

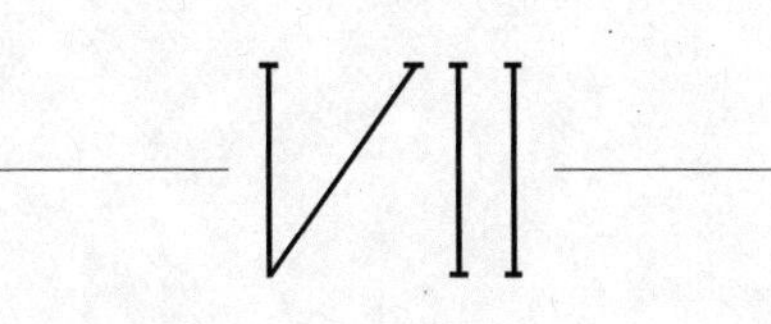

# VII

*further in*

She knows what her cousin did, eleven years ago, two years before she found out about it. She knows what it means.

If you enlist a girlfriend to promise sex as a lure to kidnap some guy.

If, when he willingly and eagerly arrives at your apartment, you beat him.

Drive him, dazed in his own car, to a scattering of ATMS.

Drag him back to the apartment.

If, fucked up on meth, you roll him into a rug.

Duct-tape it.

Bang him down two flights of steep stairs.

Heft him into the trunk of his own car.

Drive to nearby Mount Hood and dump this man, a family man, a labour lawyer who, as the celebrity journalist and all the other journalists have put it, fought for the underdog, one pro bono case after another in service to the needy, a person beloved of his community, friends, family—dear god, his family.

If you leave him.

If he's not already dead, by the next morning he will be.

The night the murdered goes missing, his wife calls the police to report it. Nothing they can do, they tell her. A person can't be officially considered missing for at least the first twenty-four hours, and did she know if he was having an affair?

Two afternoons later, a cop downtown notices the plates on the victim's car and pulls the vehicle over. Someone else is driving—surprise, Eva's cousin. The car trunk and backseat are bloodstained. He didn't even think to clean up.

The cop takes Eva's cousin in and he confesses, strikes his deal. By then it's evening. It's not until the next morning that the police notify the wife that her husband, father to their two adopted kids, is dead.

All this part of the official and public record. What Eva has read in newspapers and one magazine.

Unofficially, privately, Eva is still on the hook. Twisting and twisting. Which she has fought. Ever since she found out about her cousin's crime, and the most rational part of her, the part that most times has won out, determined she was in no way accountable. Having been out of touch with her cousin for years! How could she have known, what done?

Other times the hook sinks deeper.

She loved her cousin too much. Blinded by infatuation into failing to recognize him as a monster. Failing to raise the alarm.

Or she had not loved him enough. She abandoned him. A trauma that, piled on top of whatever else he had experienced, his mother's death in a car crash, his father's incarceration, left Eva a contributing cause of her cousin's violent deeds.

Or something shitty and vile about her drew him in and rubbed off. Something that has eluded her self-awareness. An inclination or vibe she should try to comprehend, try to change. Even now. Never too late to heal, as the latest journalist claims.

Or whatever else.

Or simply this: she had loved him. She had loved him. Guilty as charged.

# VIII

*free Eva*

She should do something. Think less, get off the couch. Text a friend and go out. Stay in and eat more. Keep her strength up.

For this?

For part of the problem is that her cousin's crime has always felt unreal. Unforeseeable back when she knew him and near-unseeable now. That he could do such a thing. That she had loved someone who could.

The other part of the problem, the flip side, is that the crime and her evident fault have felt too real. She *had* abandoned him. Lost touch the summer after their affair, when her parents began to take turns keeping her as a pawn in their ongoing battle, which divorce didn't end. Then Eva went off to college and other things.

In this formulation, she abandoned her already at-risk cousin to a lovelorn descent into drug addiction and a series of increasingly impoverished degradations and a final, horrifically brutal act.

If she were ever that important to him.

Big if, Eva.

But if she had been that important, she should have recognized the defect in him and sounded the alarm. Does her negligence not point to a defect in her, a lapse, a fault that deadened her to the evidence when she was young?

As if she'd been dead herself. As incapable of thought and action as his deceased sister. Who Eva had been jealous of! She admits it.

As if everything had been, has always been, about herself.

It shames her to think it.

If he ever had a sister, let alone a dead one. Even now Eva must remind herself that she long ago searched the birth records and came up empty-handed.

At least she has done that. At least she can feel relief that none of this shit-show is about a dead girl. Eva would scream—no, she'd roar and spit anvils, if this were another of those tales.

Having finally accepted the position of Someone Who Wants Nothing More Than For No One to Fuck With Her.

In all honesty? The worst part. Or one of the worst. About herself.

Let the record show. Although Eva has read the Victim Impact Statement, easily locatable online, read it years ago and uncovered the ambered rage located therein, the molten love trapped in stone, she has tried very hard not to think of the man her cousin killed. Or his family. She has never reached out to them. Never searched the internet for them.

She respected their privacy too much. Requiring her own—guilty as fuck.

Which she believes has to do with being unseen and unheard and confusing these with privacy. Perverting them. Converting the sense of erasure into something desirable. A fantasy of freedom. Unseen, you're free to be anyone. Free to assume other selves.

She had felt unseen from a long way back, as if rolled and taped inside the chill she experienced around her self-absorbed parents. Or at school, where she was smart enough but not the smartest.

Only her cousin seemed to recognize her, in the exclusive unfolding between them. His witness dazzled. She rode his face, his tongue between her legs, and cackled with joy. His witch, he called her. Her power, she believed.

One summer's morning someone else seemed to peg her. An emaciated man with a bruised eye and split lip, in an alleyway Eva and her cousin were cutting through. The man crooned something she couldn't make out. Jutted his hips her direction. The air reeked of tobacco and maybe human shit. She was still swollen where her cousin had earlier worked his game, entering her borrowed room and skimming into her borrowed bed the minute his stepmother's car chugged to life down the drive and onto the road. In the alley, Eva slowed and lifted her face to the cloud-flung sky above the low rooftops and felt an absence of disgust. Only curiosity. Was she walking funny? When had she last washed her hair? Why single her out?

What she suddenly understood was how easy things could be. It wouldn't be so bad to put one thing inside another inside herself, stack one Eva inside another. These Evas that certain people seemed to recognize, while a God-Eva peered from above, laughing her ass off.

A new iteration of unfolding. Or more accurately, an in-folding. In this version, nothing would need to matter very much. Not a thing. Pleasure, pain—you name it. But why bother?

She escaped, mostly through the luck of opportunity, better circumstances. Flying back east every late summer on her parents' dime. At least they remembered her enough to do that. Despite the emotional deprivations, life with her parents was in many ways one of plenty and ease. Then she went to college and found other lives for herself and eventually hit on the one she has now.

She can't seem to erase him from her head, the man in the alley with his hip thrust, his unintelligible crooning. What was it he said?

Yeah she is, her cousin called to the man, and young Eva slid back into her usual clueless self.

Is what?

Living piece of human crap, her cousin said, jutting his chin in the drunk's direction and refusing to translate.

Her cousin looped his arm around her waist, the better to steer her home.

Not Eva's home. For the record. Growing up she barely had one, even outside of summer vacation. Her parents kept threatening to chop it up along with their marriage and unload Eva at a budget version of an upstate New York boarding school. Which they did when they divorced.

It's okay, Eva: home now. Cozied in the living room. On the couch—not the nicest but not so bad. Affordable. Home where there's no one to fuck with her. Aside from the matter about the past and the matter of one fucked job. Those aside, things aren't so bad, they could be worse. She has her own bed now.

There now. She lies on top of the covers. Rain races outside and overflows the clogged eaves but she can likely scrape together enough to hire someone to clean her gutters. Be the person who realizes There Is Something She Can Do. Hire a mould remediation crew. Take better care of this house she bought thanks to her job. Which she needs to keep for as long as she can. Keep the job, her house, her modest savings. Keep her shit together. Her head.

Except her forehead is filmy and her arms clammy. Her feet sweat. Mist maid.

Song in her ears she can't name. Flu of the soul she can't name.

Sick of who she has become. She admits it. A person halfway decent and not a frequenter of alleyways. As if that's enough. To be this not quite striver who until recently has had the privilege of unfulfilling, stable work. A series of respectable relationships with non-criminal exes with whom coupling served as another kind of containment, proof against the past. As with her job, not so bad. Over time, not so great either. Her relationships sometimes fun and loving and other times messy and moderately hurtful. It took her two decades to free herself of them. Two! Decades! How's that for things adding up? Adding up to Eva sick of a certain recent Richard, that dick, Richard with his Marie for whom he abandoned Eva. Sick of the less recent Lena for whom Eva abandoned Lynn. Eva sick of the ordinary messes a person makes. She makes.

For the record, while Eva is at it: it's not just herself she's sick of. She's not so bad as all that. There is the state of the world. Global weapons sales and domestic terrorism. Children imprisoned and abused. Polar bears starving. The Amazon an inferno. Not to mention the historic and still seething oppressions in her own city. She does what she can. Attends vigils and musters small-money donations. She signs petitions and sometimes weeps at the photos she sees on social media and in the news reports. Not that her weeping helps.

Sick of thinking about the sick fuck.

This forensics of the mind. Hers but only sort of—her mind marked by him. She admits she thinks about him instead of larger things, things outside herself. Shame on her. How did she do it? Love him. Always this question. Setting aside the question of whether he ever loved her. If she were ever significant enough to have hurt him enough that he turned feral. As if that matters, given the outcomes.

Outcomes! She's also sick of feeling infiltrated by her job, contaminated by its lingo.

Sick of being a soft target for this platinum A-lister hack.

Her cousin in her soft head.

His slender back. Am I hurting you?

She yanks at the hem of her old sweater and the even older sweater beneath and lays a hand on her stomach. She imagines something clawing between the rocks of some god-forsaken shoreline to squirm beneath the surface of her skin. Another Eva. Someone Eva has endeavored to become but hasn't pulled off.

She props herself up in bed and peels off her sweaters. Her skin is slick. No joke, she should get up and take her temperature—she's too young for hot flashes. She's too sick. Contaminated. Too soft.

Not free.

Like her mother who remarried unhappily. Like Eva's father who remarried disastrously. Instead of continuing to visit her cousin on the Oregon-Washington coast, Eva shuttled between her parents on her summer breaks, her parents' bullshit stranding Eva and her cousin a silent continent apart. No writing or phoning each other, no eventually emailing or texting. A simple falling off, as happens with young people. As people do. Eva not free. Just doing stuff, turning eighteen and nineteen. In her sophomore year at college she learned through her mother—who, for a time erratically kept in touch with her brother's second wife, Eva's cousin's stepmother—that Eva's cousin had moved from Astoria to Portland. Got and lost a job. Moved to Seattle and who knew.

Eva goes over it again.

She'd been twenty-eight, the thirteen years ago when

the murder occurred. She was with Lena then. They were living in her townhouse in dull Silver Spring and Eva wasn't paying the slightest attention to people from her past. She only learned about the crime two years later, at work in DC when her mother emailed. This was still a time before any journalists had gotten even the slightest wind of Eva.

There was a link. Robbery bungler. Murderer. Dumbass meth-head. Lifer, having struck a deal to escape the death penalty Oregon still had at the time.

Eva sat at her desk in her office and took the news like the death of the cousin she had known. Cunt licker. Sweet boy.

No howls or outrage or puking. Just a quick breath. And alongside her instant grief and mourning, a wash of relief at having escaped a side of him she hadn't seen. Not really seen.

Outside her office window it was summer. DC-Baltimore humid, hot as fuck. Inside, the AC fierce. The leaves on her desk plant rattled. Someone was dead. Eva was alive. Semi-alive. Struck dumb at who he had once been to her and who she thought she'd been. Who she was until that very moment.

Was it so bad? This realignment. This death-of-self. Would it be? It was Thursday. Mid-morning. Would she cancel that day's lunch with her boss? Eva would not. She studied her plant, thought of its freshly watered roots ensconced in darkness. No, things weren't so bad on her end. She wasn't so bad. She would never discuss the case, not even with her mother, who poked about for any intel Eva might provide, before giving up.

Not free. Not even close. Not then. Not now, on top of the covers, head burning, feet like ice. How sick is that.

Where is a God-Eva when you need one? Above it all. Seeing all. Laughing at the bullshit below.

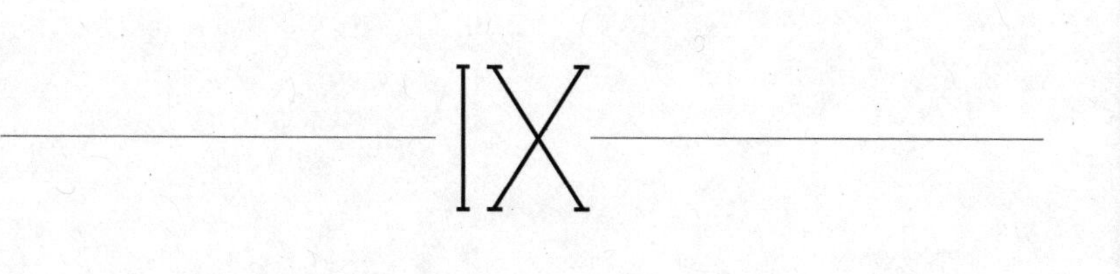

# IX

*Miss Blanky*

She's innocent, hasn't done a thing, honest. Unless she counts trying to follow the cherry of her cousin's cigarette deeper into the forest of sitkas. Off the path. She'll never find her way. She reels, weeps in circles, tugs the hem of her cut-offs. Steps on bear scat. She has to pee. A tree branch rustles and she nearly jumps out of her skin.

She wakes in her bathroom, on the toilet. The water-stained walls uphold her—she isn't sporing into the earth's atmosphere and tainting it as the dead do. She is in her bathroom. She is on the toilet, peeing. Rain falls on the roof. The window steams. Her bladder loosens and empties. She is forty-one and not a girl and most certainly not a Dead Girl.

In her bedroom again, Eva presses her face into the pillow. She has thought of her cousin over the years. She has. Before the murder and since. Pale thoughts, little fogs. They enter through her left nostril and cool her, depart without a trace through her right. Cold fires. She curls into a ball and stretches, rearranges her limbs. This angle, that. Every joint aches. The rain sluices down the bedroom window. Her thoughts a foul paste. If she could wash them away, see what's missing. A clouded mirror. The fog clears. She is missing.

She can't tell if she misses him. Misses their time together. She wonders if he's still alive, if prison has killed him. No way would she like to see him again. No fucking way. No: he could be alive, dead, for all she knows and cares. Alive, dead, one, zero. Like candy hearts that click together in her head. In her head like young Click and Clack blazed and atilt up the hill to the old house where nobody can ever find them. Missing together. Missing like his dead sister, exactly like his sister, who nobody can find. Not without photos or birth or death records. This other Little Miss Blanky.

The woods again, deeper in. How far to fill in the blanks? Very far: she reaches, moans, spreads wide, stretches so hard her neck might snap and her head roll off. She might need it though—for god's sake, Eva, there's a book to finish reading. Friends to text. A droll amazement to feel at still having a couple-few friends. Eva, ease the fuck up! Things aren't so bad, why make things worse?

Some other time! She's busy, very. Working her fingers like her cousin's superior ass play.

She gets off but not in a big way and minnows into sleep. And for her next trick, dreams. But how boring.

She wakes and it's still Thursday, kill her now. She rouses and heads downstairs to the dark kitchen and stands in the light from the open fridge. She devours the leftover noodles. Grease and salt swell her gums and she recalls her cousin boiling hot dogs. The salty rime. He chewed tidily, eating three to her one then pawing his mouth with his sleeve. Sweat on his upper lip. She can almost taste him now. The irresistible loneliness, much like her own, that glazed his pores.

She licks her own lips before catching herself and wishing to unlick them.

No undoing what is done.

What she has missed.

She has missed a lot. She hasn't had a clue.

To be honest, a clue is what she needs. A shit-ton's worth.

A way to understand why she feels responsible for his fate. Why she indulges this feeling of complicity. What she gains by it aside from clit boners and a sense of her own fate, chosen to nearly die and chosen to live.

Aside from the grandiosity of feeling she has a fate.

Aside from this desire to cling to feeling loved by him once—to believe that if she truly is complicit, if her abandoning him left a vacuum that led to his destructive spiral, it means he truly loved her.

For god's sake, Eva! Will you just wash the chopsticks

and put them away. Rinse the take-out container and drop it in the recycling.

With a head loose as rain. The spaces between drops. Her cousin in her head, his smile in her head. His tongue in her cunt in her head.

She runs the dishwasher though there is no need.

If she does lose her job. If she loses her best defenses. Getting let go, letting go. Released to the flattery of still feeling loved by her cousin. The flattery wielded by the journalist in service of rehearsing an old tale. Rehearsing her old role within that tale. Her part shaped by her cousin, before and after the murder. Her part in her cousin's story. A piece of a puzzle jammed in. Forced to fit.

Her cousin in her head.

In her living room she drags her laptop onto her lap like a not very bright pet. At least it's no sly fox in a dumb cold book.

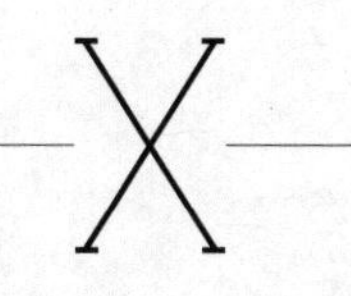

# *departures*

Three weeks later Eva is at BWI. Live it up, Eva. Two uncharacteristic early morning Bloody Marys and a Klonopin at the sports bar near her gate. A double-shot decaf Americano in a to-go cup. She finds a seat near her crowded gate and faces the tarmac where planes slumber under a punchy blue sky. After weeks of rain, the change in weather feels like a reproach for her sudden and vaguely explained leave of absence from work, for her purchase of perilously expensive tickets. For her thinking, in a likely lapse of judgment, that she should travel while she still has income.

She hates flying. Detests airports. A young couple seated nearby argue loudly and viciously over whose fault it is that they've forgotten their bagged lunches. A toddler trips near Eva and hauls itself up, sticky hands on Eva's jeans. A face-masked and latex-gloved security guard stationed by the gate's check-in counter surveys the waiting travellers, some of whom, Eva realizes, are coughing and blowing noses. She hurries to a kiosk and stocks up on hand sanitizer, headache pills, vitamin C.

Too soon Eva buckles into her seat in 21A and submits to takeoff, quaking like a dying beast's guts in a terrible movie. The plane soars and airport and roadways and suburbs and farmland and fields squeeze flat as road-kill, as if crushed by the weight of her fear of vast heights. All that space beneath her. To fall into. To float above.

On the flip side, her fear of tightly enclosed spaces, fear of germs.

She grips her armrests. It's too soon for another drink—the flight attendants snugged in tight, leaving Eva to enumerate other anxieties.

Fear she might atomize in an ether of dismay when her snoring seatmate droops his head to her shoulder and pins her.

Fear at the prospect of crappy movies and fear caused by crappy movies. Though not those depicting airplane peril, those are never shown on planes, peril such as a demon surfing alongside a passenger's window. Like Eva's own. And no one on board to believe her.

She releases her grip on the armrests and flips down the window shade. The plane reaches cruising altitude and the flight attendants wheel their trolley. Another Bloody Mary. A small bag of roasted peanuts. The minor consolations. Except the foil packet is Eva-proof. She cannot for the life of her open it. Proof of the existence of the pure algebraic universe—the more she struggles, the more she has never before wanted anything so badly.

Fear of starvation for want of a single peanut.

A quick re-up on the drink. A robust one, yes, another Bloody Mary. To stave off starvation and the beast that clings to the fuselage outside Eva's window, the creature's claws stronger than whatever aircraft are constructed from.

Stronger than Eva's fears at twelve, thirteen, fifteen.

Fear of her mother abandoning her and her father. Fear of her father getting jailed like her cousin's father, Eva's mother's brother.

Fear of Eva's mother dead in a car crash like her cousin's mother, and Eva's father remarrying and then jailed.

Eva left with a stepmother she wouldn't care to know—her cousin's plight. Cousin who claimed to have this dead sister who passed years earlier. From asthma, he revealed after two summers of Eva pestering him. From breathing and then not. And Eva jealous of the sister, who had her brother all to herself until she died. Eva scared of the sister's ghost on storm nights. Scared when the floorboards of the old house on the hill creaked at night, storm or not. A creaking ghost-sister jealous of Eva. Sister who might crush Eva to a pulp between ghostly hands turned horned and clawed.

Eva polishes off her drink and panic-sips the grubby air. She flips up her window shade, the better to face her enemy.

Midday. Blue skies. Not so bad.

Until it is. Reflected in the plexi, her own fear-contorted, oxygen-starved face peers back at her.

Fear of returning and fear of not. Eva suspended between them.

Fear of returning to face an avenging harpy, a creepy old house on a hill, an old woman unhappy to see Eva. A top-shelf journalist happy to feast on Eva's vanity and ignorance and her desire to know about her cousin, and herself. All that.

Fear of not returning. Not uncovering—what?

How bad can it be?

Another drink, please.

If she can stop digging her nails into her arms, surreptitiously, beneath her sweater's sleeves. If her seatmate will unbuckle and head to the bathroom, and she can seize the opportunity to grab her tote from beneath the seat in front of her. If she can score her book, ferret out her phone. Hit her pranayama app. Insert ear buds and drift.

Had he or had he not had other girlfriends? Before Eva. After her. Or boyfriends—why not?

He could not possibly be Eva's sole responsibility.

Her cousin in her head.

Once again facedown on the beach, feet from the waterline. Dark sand masks the backs of his thighs and there's a stiff breeze, goosebumps all over again, a radio beside him but no sound except the thundering waves of the incoming tide. Sleeping? She should let him know the tide is coming in. She should. Before the late afternoon crisps to starless night. The waters rise.

Her seatmate unbuckles and heads to the bathroom.

If Eva can hold on, wait. Remain in her seat and close her eyes and see how things end.

Her cousin, on his back now, looking up. Smiling! The little shit.

The flight attendants wheel their trolley again and Eva will have a crappy coffee, thank you. She opens the book on her lap. Where was she?

The captain says, A smooth ride all the way in, folks.

It's only afternoon, Pacific time. Snow-capped spires fret beneath the plane's slow descent and soon the great river emerges like a lush, recurring dream.

The captain comes on again and apologizes. She misspoke. Excuse her. Folks, looks like we've got a little weather ahead of us.

At the final approach to PDX a hard rain cloaks the view.

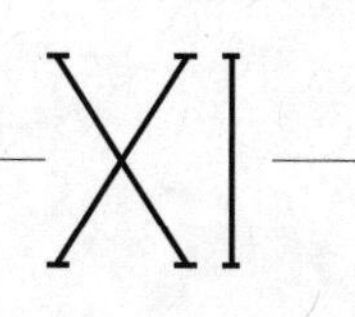

# XI

*arrival*

Eva overnights in Portland. She purchases some weed at a dispensary and treats herself to a fancy dinner. The next day she drives her rental north to Astoria and checks into a hotel near the befogged river, belts her trench coat and stalks the misty streets. She inhales an excellent late breakfast in a local-organic-fare café. Reminded of how her cousin had liked her skinny, she orders two pastries to go. She buys a green silk scarf at a boutique for her boss, Tina. At an artisans' atelier, for Tina's daughter Eva buys a handmade wooden pull duckie. She settles on a city bench and digs into the pastries, marvels at all the brewpubs and expensive AWDs. Then she strolls up into the residential streets where elegantly restored houses gleam through the silvery light. Carefully pruned azaleas pop in yards and colourful murals banner garage doors.

She feels a measure of pride, and then disappointment. She has travelled this far, away and now back, to discover she has been left behind, like a hollow shell washed by shallow waves.

She finds some comfort in what hasn't changed. The riverine breeze. Glimpses of freighters and tugs through the mist and fog, plying their trade on the waterways below, leaving wakes like giant diesel-scented eels. Across the truss bridge and the state line to Washington and the peninsula, the forests dark.

By late afternoon she summons her courage and locates the old place.

She claps a hand to her mouth to keep from crying out in delight. The cracked and flaking exterior paint. Untrimmed hedges, the patchy lawn. The same as she remembered. Her mood lifts.

There are signs of improvement though, which she regards with suspicion. The shaky porch replaced. Curtains rather than bed sheets over the living room windows. A newish aqua-coloured economy car in the paved drive that once was dirt. A tuxedo cat grooms itself by the front door. The tabby Eva's cousin sometimes gifted saucers of milk must have been dead for years now.

Eva climbs the porch steps and knocks. She regrets operating this way, her arrival unannounced, but her stepmother's number remains unlisted and there's no trace of her online. Eva could have circled back with the journalist and enquired—she still could, if she needs to, if the woman has relocated—but then Eva would feel like she was admitting a win for him.

She would, however, like to know how he found the woman. Why she would have talked to him, and not to the others that came sniffing around all those years ago. Wherever she might be—Eva has been so hopeful of late, so self-involved, that she had largely discounted the possibility that the stepmother would not be here. What will Eva say to the occupant if the woman has moved on? Eva raps her fists against her temples. What will she say if the old lady does live here? If she answers the door?

Mister Tux investigates her calves. Eva can hardly stand it, can hardly stand her own questions and is about to creep away when a shape approaches the other side of the screen door.

Now what? a voice says.

Through the screen the woman shakes her head at the name Eva offers, scans her tip to toe. The door swings. Bare feet swollen beneath loose pants. A yank at the front of the baggy tee. The old woman jams her neck into her thick shoulders. Her face is swollen and red.

I'm not talking to you, she says. I don't know you.

Eva doesn't recognize her either—well, sort of, but not really. Hardly a surprise. Her cousin's stepmother had seemed like a clumsy piece of furniture occasionally taken from storage and again dragged out of sight. Eva winces. Apologize? In case this really is her cousin's stepmother. And how would Eva even begin?

The woman opens her mouth as if to speak again and lets it hang. As if she too has things on her mind and no idea where to start.

It was years ago, Eva says, forging ahead on a keen hunch, or simply her racing desire for this to be the right person. I spent summers here with you. You and my cousin. You spoke with a journalist about me?

The woman stares through Eva. Wrong person. Or the right one but no help. Or worse than that—the old bat set Eva up with the journalist and refuses to acknowledge it. Some kind of fucked up game. But why?

Her vision shakes like a fist shaking dice. A bird chucks from the nearest bush and the cat pounces off the porch after it and Eva really should go too. She shifts her weight, embarrassed, thwarted into helplessness. But she wants in. So much. The sense is overpowering, not only of her desire, but of her right—to walk the old floorboards and slouch against the kitchen counter and lie down in a bed that doesn't belong to her. To haunt. Imagine the past so fully as to inhabit who she was back then. Who he was. To feel at home in that past. Home. To imagine feeling so loved—there it is, here she is. Still here wanting his love.

Now a great urge to sleep overtakes her. Syrupy. Yes, she did have a gummy earlier. Yes, the jet lag.

Appallingly, she feels a pinch in her groin.

The woman breathes audibly and holds her ground.

You old bitch, Eva's cousin growls in her head—and she feels ashamed that she's able to eavesdrop on his ancient curses.

I've come all this way, she blurts.

The woman lifts her chin and freezes. She drops her chin a fraction in the slightest of nods. It occurs to Eva that she might have misremembered the stepmother's name and that this is the reason Eva was unable to contact her. The woman's name! Why should she spare an expression of reluctant pity or the faintest interest in Eva? Beyond telling the journalist about her. Which she did because? To shift his interest, and the possibility of any longstanding blame, from herself to Eva?

Get the fuck out of here, Eva. Go, now. Let go.

She steps back and Eva's cousin's stepmother emits a ragged cough, coughs so hard tears ooze from her eyes.

Can I do anything? A glass of water? I can run in to the kitchen and get you—

The battle-axe, the great big—she holds up a hand. A few more seconds and she catches her breath. Uses both hands to fan the air in front of her.

She says, You said you were who?

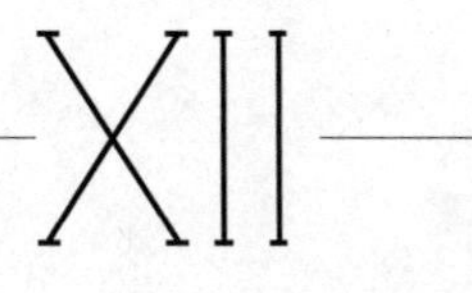

*Eva meets the old woman again*

The next morning Eva and Ruth sit across from each other sipping coffee in a diner. Eva is not blazed, as she was yesterday and last night. Still fuzzy though. Not only the weed and jet lag but also the strangeness of walking streets at once familiar and unrecognizable—as if a second map has been overlaid atop a first, off by a slim, uncanny margin.

Eva needs to find her footing and fast. She needs to get Ruth to look at her instead of continuing to glare out the diner's window at the river by the far eastern end of town, near the out-of-business lumberyard. Nearer the channel, to the west, rollers bash the shore. The bridge to Washington State rises like a huge mechanical snake. Tomorrow Eva will drive across that bridge and pick the journalist's brain, use him for her own ends. For now, Eva has tough old Ruth, and Eva must conceal a hideous old anger at feeling displaced. She needs to get Ruth to spill some fucking beans. That would semi make up for not letting Eva in the house yesterday. A situation she hopes to rectify today.

Thank you for seeing me, she says and nudges the plate of two muffins forward.

Ruth turns to face Eva squarely and shoves the plate back. She struggles to match this person to the mostly silent, absent woman she remembers. This one looks like she'd tear off her own head for using too much toilet paper.

Here's what I have to tell you, Ruth says. All I got.

Eva feels a jolt of anticipation, half relief and half fear.

I appreciate it.

Don't thank me yet, Ruth says, scowling. All I'm telling is that it's been tough. I've had to chase all them away. Put an end to their questions.

Heat builds behind Eva's eyes. Old cow, she can almost hear her cousin mutter.

Fuck, Eva. Dial it back. Imagine the pressures of Ruth's financial situation. Not impossible to imagine landing in similar straits. Think of what blows Ruth has withstood. Husband in prison until he died of renal failure. Stepson in prison—the weight of what he did. A burden of guilt ten-fold what Eva might feel.

I'm sorry you had to go through that, Eva says, and she means it, she is sorry. A few got in touch with me too. And I did what you did. Got rid—

Look here, Ruth says. *Eva.* If that's who you say you are. I don't remember you at all. I thought I did for a moment yesterday. But today you're a big nope. Maybe a snoop.

Might as well try to budge a statue. In fact, now that Eva thinks back again, she realizes that when Ruth wasn't working, she had seemed less a piece of furniture and more a mineral chunk stashed in cheap blankets, supine on the couch. Silent, but mean. A bulk behind her closed bedroom door, sounds of her TV gravelling under the crack at the bottom. A rock gnashing a couple of frozen dinners in the kitchen and not offering Eva or her cousin anything to eat. Bringing the dinners home each night, only enough for herself, in a small grocery bag. How had Eva forgotten? The fridge mostly empty, except for what Eva's cousin's odd jobs could afford, and the small allowance for Eva's upkeep that her parents sometimes remembered to wire. Eva would open and close the fridge over and over, just checking. The interior light out. The dim shapes of expired bottles of ketchup and mayo. Musty smell. Her cousin liked her skinny anyways.

Eva's cousin skinny too.

The fridge door shuts in Eva's head, a car door swings open, the interior irradiated. Eva's cousin nuzzles her ear and she fingers the collar on his shirt and he does that thing he does, his mouth on her neck, nipples, belly, devouring his way south. Her mouth starving away at his shoulders, whatever skinny parts she can stuff herself on.

Nope, Eva cannot leave. She's spent years shutting the car door and now it's flung wide. The engine races. Her hair blows around her head and ignites like fireflies. She is No Big Nope.

Ruth reaches for the plate of muffins with a grunt. She peels the wax paper from one, cuts the muffin in two with her knife and butters it. Two bites per half and they're gone. She presses a finger to the crumbs.

Why did you even agree to meet with me today? Eva snaps. Why are you still in Astoria? You could have cashed in.

Today? Ruth says with a flick of her brows. And why are *you* here? If you're who you say you are. Because you could be another Eva, couldn't you. Trying to cash in yourself. And if you are her, seems like you never left either. Since here you are.

Fireflies. Eva's cousin's palms pressed into her bucking hips. His attentions did their trick for her once, elevated her. But she hardly needs a nostalgia for his tricks now, hardly needs to still be that person who needed them.

She will be another Eva now. She Who Needs To Know. Who Can Sort Things Out. Who Is Finally Old Enough To Know. As if this is her true vocation.

Can you tell me how old I was back then—can Eva ask that?

Ruth tears a napkin from the napkin dispenser, makes a show of swiping her chin and lips. She balls the napkin and bounces it to the plate next to the uneaten muffin.

If you really want to know, Ruth says, I'm still here because it's home. You know, where the heart is? If that makes sense to the likes of you. Anyways, that's all you'll get from me.

She crosses her arms over her chest, looking pleased with herself. Slappable face on her.

Eva cannot ask.

Nor can she ask other questions. Why did you give this journalist my name? Did you know about my cousin and I, and not do anything about it? Until now. Now that the journalist is paying you for information? Is he in fact paying you?

The old bitch resettles her butt on her booth seat and leans toward Eva. There is someone else you could ask, she says. A reporter.

Thanks, Eva says in a flat voice, uncertain if Ruth's new tack proves Eva's suspicions. Generous of you. I already have plans to see him tomorrow.

Ruth startles. The Jew boy? she says.

Eva puffs air through her nose. The journalist, she says, speaking slowly to over-emphasize the word, as if correcting a child. The famous one. You told him about me? Did you forget? I'm going to his house.

Ruth appears to take this in stride, laying her hands palm down in front of her on the table.

Okay, she says. Here's the deal. I can tell you this. You're really in for something. That place is something to see.

You know it?

I clean it.

Eva is surprised and then not. I can't believe you're not retired yet, she snipes, realizing that Ruth likely can't afford to quit working.

Ruth stares at her chapped hands. She must be well into her seventies. She will likely need to work until she drops of a heart attack or stroke, or cancer or kidney failure fells her.

A real character, that one, Ruth says, recovered and suddenly seeming happy to display her insider knowledge. Likes to play dress-up, she says. Claims his book's classy. Not trying to make money off people's misery.

He said that to me too. He—

Like maybe you are, Ruth snaps back. Out for the misery-money.

I'd be so grateful, Eva says fastidiously, aware of her lack of subtlety but pressing on anyway, one cunt to another. Truly grateful, she says. Truly, for whatever else you could tell me. Or show me. Do you have old photos? At the house?

A belly laugh. Ruth's eyes seem to roll up into her head.

Grateful my ass, she says, and wipes her face with her hand. You wouldn't be, if you were the old Eva. That little bitch. But go ahead, sweetie. Prove to yourself you're for real. Keep knocking yourself out.

# XIII

*for whom*

Another pill, a pre-rolled, two glasses of wine. Not so bad. Until she settles into her hotel bed and a memory of sleep but not the thing itself. Old things. They slice into the room and bring wind and rain that needle her face. She tries not to move or call out. The murdered man beside her in bed. Then fast black and she is outside the room and rain caresses hedges and bridges and the house on a hill from which, aside from her memories, she is eternally barred. Someone else's home, never hers. The old anxiety a cold wave. The city below glows green through the fog. Rain runnels down streets and alleys and sticks to her hands and she is suddenly in her kitchen. It is years later. Her fingers are sticky. Sour smell. Steam gushes from a pot. She is in her kitchen, overcooking the eggs. Broken eggs. A laugh foams inside her, her jaw clunks sideways, she bites her tongue awake. Alone. The room dark with hours. Old things. A clouded mirror. Am I hurting you? Out on the river, channel buoys toll the night.

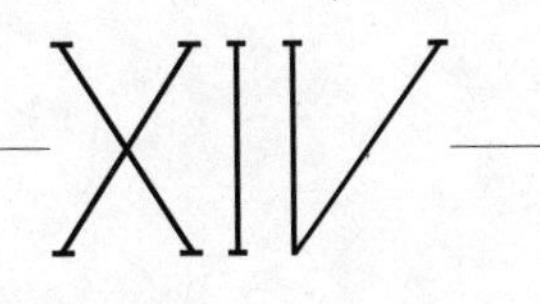

*Eva learns her cousin's true fate*

Under cauldron skies the next morning an exhausted Eva drives her rental across the truss bridge. She takes the peninsula's secondary road past cranberry bogs and sitkas and beech. Mounds of pink and red azaleas still grow wild by the roadside. To the east she glimpses the glass-surfaced bay with its heron rookery and oyster farms. On clear days there's a distant view of Mount Rainier to the north. New road signs greet her. TSUNAMI EVACUATION ROUTE. GOOD TIDES ORGANIC FARM GOAT CHEESE DROP IN MEET THE KIDS. She takes a smaller road west and stops at the general store in Ocean Park, the peninsula's largest town, and picks out a local craft beer and a decent wine—improbable propositions years ago. She drops the goods off in the car and walks a block to the beach. One of Eva and her cousin's spots, though usually they took up farther north where few people braved the heavy gusts and pounding surf.

Wind-shot sand. A weather-beaten plaque. RIP TIDES NO SWIMMING. A solitary eagle hunches on a dead branch and sanderlings inscribe the water's lacy edge with probing beaks. The surf bangs and she feels it inside, where her cousin's cock banged her cervix. Way in. Bang bang. Can't get him out.

She waits. Thunder booms. A door opens in the pavilion and the journalist appears carrying a large black umbrella. He is short and thick and wearing a black leather jacket. He raps on the window with an elbow and she buzzes down. Rain splashes in.

He says, Hello chicken.

The downpour stops, the sound replaced by a racket of hummingbirds. They beat, like bejewelled hearts on speed, at the seven feeders that line the covered deck off the dining room. Beyond the deck the bay is so still it appears to levitate. The journalist, who goes by the name Dash, uncorks a bottle and pours two glasses. He holds his high, waves it at Eva. To you, she thinks he says above the thicket of sound. She thinks he says that the wife he is sick of banging is in Dubai, dean of an Ivy's abroad program. The mayor of Baltimore these days is? You've lived there how long?

She answers the questions she thinks he asks and he gulps and splashes on himself unapologetically, bullishly, at odds with the wisps of pink-dyed hair tendrilled to his waxy scalp. His lips are thick and mobile though, as are his large brown eyes and smooth high forehead, and he punctuates her replies with snorts through his pudgy nose. He has yet to remove his richly studded leather jacket, and when he waves his hands to speak, his wrists appear, circled by chunky metal cuffs. The jacket occasionally gapes open to reveal a form-fitting slashed tee, a soft midriff above leather pants stubbed into designer-logo-emblazoned motorcycle boots. He looks her up and down, and she tries to stand taller, to not shrink from him. She wonders if he's even heard her responses to his questions.

What do you think, Eva? she thinks he says, tipping his glass toward the bay. A toast to my resplendent view?

The living room also overlooks the bay and here there is a large sectional and two elaborately carved chairs. Chinese throne chairs, Qing Dynasty, early eighteenth century, he points out, along with other Asian antiques. He points out the important European and American mid-century pieces and pulls a catalogue off a shelf and hands it to her, stands very close and nudges her shoulder with his.

Eva flips pages. She came for this? His performed expertise as he explains that the Japanese erotic photographs evolved from the shunga tradition. That shunga means "spring pictures." Woodblock prints depicting sex acts, eighteenth to the early twentieth centuries. Also called higa, "secret pictures." Some were done in series that conveyed stories.

His cologne smells like gasoline laced with something sweet. She knows what she should do, elbow him in the gut, tell him to back the fuck off. Resist wanting to humour him in the service of finding out what he knows, not about an esoteric erotic tradition, his interest in it exoticizing, but about her cousin—as if that could shed light on herself.

Bad idea to come here, Eva. Very bad. She should hurry herself the fuck back home and carry her dismay and embarrassment with her. A home of her own—she has that now. She should never have left it.

But she came all this way. This is his show. She will

stay and observe him at work. Even though what he's working on at the moment is her. Trying to intimidate, unsettle. Set her up.

This one, he says, inserting his index finger between two pages.

He takes her by the elbow and guides her toward a portion of the wall above the sectional. The same photo from the catalogue is elegantly matted and framed. A squatting woman fingering herself. Another page, another photo in the flesh, this one above a throne chair. Two men and a woman intertwined, sucking and fucking.

The old shunga images, he explains. Created by the artists of the ukiyo-e or floating world school of the seventeenth through nineteenth centuries. *Ukiyo* also a homophone for sorrowful world.

So what do you think, Eva? he says. Sorrowful world?

She closes the catalogue and drops it on the sectional. Refuses to rise to his bait.

A kind of graphic storytelling, he says. In both senses. Looking at them helps give me ideas. Helps me confront the deepest darkest. What we usually hide. How about you? What helps you?

He drapes an arm around her shoulder, squeezes. Her heart skips several beats.

Eva, Eva. Here you are. Here. You. Are. I'm so fucking glad.

He knocks his left temple, gently, against her right. Then he indicates her wine glass, which she has deposited on a side table.

Now drink the fuck up, Eva. Enough rubbernecking, okay? Ixnay on the nostalgia for the old days, right? We have business to attend to.

He watches her drink then takes her glass with the flourish of a skilled headwaiter fussing at his staff's negligence, and deposits it on a console.

Here, he says, gesturing grandiloquently toward the far end of the ample room.

The desk faces the water and is stacked with files and books. Eva draws near. The spines spell out addiction, class relations, mental disorders.

It all happens here, he says. The magic.

Is it working now? she says.

A look of surprise on his face.

You tell me, Eva.

She mimics his expression and his eyes grow cold and hard.

Eva, he says, lowering his voice. I've been looking for you a long time. And now that you're here, tell me something. Tell me everything you know.

He touches her elbow again and his touch this time is firmer. His face looms close to hers and for a second she fears he might kiss her. She is afraid to move away, show she is weak, that she is afraid of him.

No kiss. Just his thick, mobile lips near her ear.

Ready, Eva? Wanna roll?

That it? That all you got?

They're back in the living room, seated. He flings an arm over the top of the sectional and crosses a leg over a knee. He exhales loudly and slowly.

What are you, he continues. A crazy lady? No dead sis. No sis, period. If there had been, I would've tracked her down. Dead girls are easy to trace. Especially the pretty white ones. Bonus points if they come from nice homes. Okay, that last bit not the case in this case, and maybe the first bit too wouldn't have been the case. Anyway, good on you to make that one up. I like the bestseller in that. Pure fiction, like it's never been done before. That's a joke, chicken. But okay, say I like your imagination. That's some show where your head goes. I really like your shit. It could lead places. Care to share some more?

Excuse me? Eva says, barely stopping herself from raising her hand. I have a question.

She has already embarrassed herself, asking after her cousin's made-up dead sister—just in case. That out of the way, she can relax, ask away.

He rolls his eyes, then checks his chunky watch and exhales showily again.

Okay. Shoot.

Why now? The book you're writing. Isn't it old news?

For Christ's sake. Might as well ask yourself, Evie. For your bestseller-in-progress. Your lurid tell-all.

Ha, she says. Good one. Another one on me.

He examines her as if gauging her crushability.

Also, she says. How did you even know about me? How did you get Ruth to talk at all?

Shit, he says, uncrossing his legs and bouncing his knees, looking everywhere around the room but at Eva, clearly bored. That's just fucking tradecraft. Sorry to bust your idea of yourself as some glamorous masked woman.

He rubs his jaw and she can hear his day-old bristle.

But look, Eva? Hello? Speaking to your first question, why now? That's a good one. It's just that the nefarious stupid crime your darling cousin committed, he was darling, right? Okay, I get it, game face on. You're tough, you know that? You're breaking me, breaking my I-won't-say, and that's out of respect for my mother, may her memory be a blessing. Anyway, the evil deed for which your cousin's a lifer in the federal pen, just to fucking remind you, did happen a lucky thirteen years ago. Old news. Old, rotten, stinking news. You're right on that score. Except we're in a moment. You must have noticed. Sex and drugs and co-dependence, a good man gone bad, gone dead. I should say a white man, an affluent man. One fuck up and he gets wasted by a baddie. Who is, who was, bad for reasons, a compelling backstory. I get that, I can empathize. That's the secret ingredient for any writer, you need to know that, Evie, if you don't already. Anyway, throw it all together, shake and pour. Class and gentrification and a troubled childhood. But the best part, I'm getting to that. There's sex too, am I right? Sexual harassment, illegal sex. Sex abuse. Eva, that's even more of the moment.

He takes a breath while continuing to scrutinize her.

Eva, am I right? Sticky fingers with a minor?

Okay, he says. I get it, we just met. First date. Anyway. Voilá, rock 'n roll. It's all opening up, everyone wants to know. Don't you? I mean, aside from yourself, your own experiences. Aren't you having a moment? What are you, forty? Don't tell me. Forty-eight-nine? Not sure if the math works, but just going by looks.

He clasps a knee with his interlaced fingers and shrugs.

Okay, he says. Okay, so your cousin's story. It's societally important to know. You know?

He unclasps his hand from his knee and slaps his thigh, like he's acting out some high comedy for her.

Shit, he says. Come on, Eva. I think you're holding out on me.

He says, How old were you when it went down? So to speak.

He says, Think of me as your friend, Eva. I'll be as respectful as fuck. What can you tell me about what happened to you, sweetie? I mean, holy crap you didn't come all this way to ask about a dead sister, did you?

That's some game you're trying to diddle me with, he says.

He says, Or yourself.

He says, Allow me to enlighten you. Nostalgia will never set you free. I'd hate to see you learn the hard way. Amend that. I'm hating to see it. But I can. I can see it. You are so fucked up. Have to be, to hop on that plane, shoot on out here. Come on, Eva. What's in that tight-assed head of yours?

A single raindrop. Silver seed. It falls through tree branches while Eva waits, takes her time. She waits and fog rolls in. Steam rises from a bath. She waits for the fog to clear.

I'll tell you what's in mine, he says. In case you really, really want to know. Your Romeo? At this point, he's just fodder for the masses. Semi-instructive, at best. The best that the little bastard can be now. A cautionary flash-point. Because for reals? The little turd is buried so deep in the pen he'll never get out. Not with the forty-six years before he's eligible for parole. You don't think he'll be dead by then? You know the girlfriend got twenty-four?

He says, With good behavior, she could be out any day now.

Anyway, I go to see him, he says. Did you know? But you haven't. That's not you, right, chicken? You bailed years ago. Good on you. So look at you, the great redemption narrative herself. I mean, look how well you turned out. And that right there, Eva, that's your story, the one I'll print, make it nice and tidy, make you happy. I can make you very, very happy, Eva.

More rain. Warm on her cold skin. The sensation giddying. She can get what she wants. What does she want? To keep going. Keep going. Keep getting him going and see where it all lands. She has this, if she wants it. Does she want it?

Eva rouses herself. I like how you put things, she says. Really, I do.

He gives her a look of pure disgust.

Cut the bull, Eva. Pretty please?

She says, Question. Is there more wine?

Fuck no, my dear. There is no more fucking wine. You're cut off. We have arrived at this point, our cozy impasse. I need you to understand. This is what you need to know. What I can offer. I can do this one thing for you, one old pro to another. I can lift a finger, I can make that call. And like that, you can see your precious cousin for yourself. I mean tomorrow. If you so desire. Bottom line, isn't that your heart's desire? Why you came all this way? Surely not to see this glamorous mug. Right? What do you think of that, Eva?

Maybe I was just bored.

Maybe, he says, putting air quotes around the word with his fingers.

They're both silent for a moment.

Otherwise, he says, ramming on again. Otherwise, without my call to pull a string or two, it's just protocols up the asshole. You'd have to wait weeks to get a response. The go-ahead to pay a nice visit, yack up the fond memories. Weeks. Fuck, even then, I'm just saying, even then. And besides, he might veto your request, he has that right. Maybe he'd turn you down, Eva.

I mean, Dash says. If you really want to see him, I could help.

He says, Because I'm picking up a certain vibe here. I bet you loved him. And you don't know what to do with it. Do you?

He says, Let's just say I scratch your itch, you scratch mine.

*for whom*

Eva walks the narrow trail running alongside the pristine estuary. Pristine! her journo pal insisted. Thanks to him, on account of his spearheading restoration efforts. His masterful ability to prevent these boonies from backsliding.

Eva walks, another kind of waiting. The sun has resurfaced and the mountain shows to the north, the bay a silver disc. Everything she does, a form of waiting. She snaps off a stalk of sea bean and chews. Salt and iodine flood her mouth, sting her lungs. She marvels again: what used to be free nosh now garnishes dishes in fancy west coast restaurants, she's learned from the past several evenings she has spent living some other life. A more spendy, indulgent one featuring good wine and good food and whatnot—Klonopins and joints smoked beneath the awnings of much fancier hotels than the one Eva is staying at. Another Eva, growing plump, blank as the oysters and clams in these pure waters, captive in their mud beds to someone else's expertly curated dreaming.

Eva shakes her head. This guy. A workshop in getting what he wants. As she expected, and far worse.

Like her cousin. A master at getting what he wanted from Eva when she was young. Marking her. Inhabiting, contaminating. Miss me, think of me.

She comes to the end of the path, shades her eyes with her hand. This place, tame and lovely. She and her cousin rarely ventured here all those years ago, preferring the oceanside, wind and currents, dead seals.

What *is* she waiting for?

A sudden finger of joy crazes deep in her gut seconds before it reaches her throat and she croaks a laugh—it's not so bad. To be beside herself. Walking, waiting. Not so bad to spy across the water a small detail, a prick of shade. Her cousin. His cock out. Taking a piss.

# XVI

*Eva drives and arrives, singing*

My Bonnie Lies Over the Ocean. Head Like a Hole. Gloria, Rid of Me, Woke Up Weird. For Eva is no girl and certainly not a dead one and she is old enough to indulge a safe nostalgia in songs of her own choosing. A nostalgia safe as driving the speed limit on this rare, utterly clear day, south and away from the great river's mouth, with its subsea canyons and sweeping tidal flow and turbulent currents—according to her hotel brochure, the most treacherous waters for ships on the Pacific coast.

Safe as averting her eyes from Mount Hood, visible to the east past Portland. Another hour's driving and she'll arrive in Salem, a law-and-order place. Safe as how she owes no one anything. Not even Dash the journalist. Dash! for god's sake. Sharpie who pulled strings in an arrangement she shook hands on yesterday and has no plans of honouring. The asshole can eat it.

Liar, cheat, she drives, just drives. Let's go. My Bonnie Lies. Head Like a Hole. She slaps the steering wheel in time, head bangs. Let's go, spitting boulders and ocean crust. She peers, as if from above with a God-eye, on her much younger knees purple from crawling Astoria's South Jetty rocks, fingertips scraped raw trying to keep up with her cousin. Once upon a time. Hurts. Drives with her suitcase in the rental's trunk and nothing more, knows what her cousin did and why Dash is so interested. Why the others were. Bullshit. All is bullshit. Never Forget, Never Repeat. This Magic Moment. My Bonnie Lies.

Eva pulls into a parking spot. Beyond the windshield, not a cloud in the sky. The brightness stark, not so bad. Balls to the Wall. She spanks that steering wheel. No clit boners. No avenging, winged shape. Only Eva here. Herself by herself. She has done the deal with Dash and he has quickly pulled strings, not really for her but for his own purposes, she understands that. For the exclusive she has promised—but she is only Eva here. She owes no one. He can go fuck. My Bonnie Lies. She owes only who she will be when she meets her cousin again and who she will be after.

She is in a time before other times, she believes that. The rain, the wind, have softened her, allowed her to believe, allowed this brilliant day to cement it.

Over the Ocean! Head Like a Hole.

The lot stretches as if for miles.

The door flung open. In park with her foot to the gas, gunning it as if under a thousand suns flooding a million empty cars. She turns off the engine and sniffs. It's hotter and drier here than on the coast. She climbs out and slams the door shut. Surveys this new realm as if she has created it. Chrome and glass in endless replication, honeycombed at noon, dripping light.

# XVII

*Eva learns her own true fate*

Who are you, again? Eva's cousin says across the partition.

Eva hates the gasp that gasses from her throat. She hates his response, a cruel mirror intake of breath. She hates that she thought to apply lipstick. Hates that his lips swish into a smile like a cat's tail. As if she has given him a present. As if she has come in his fucking mouth.

His fucking mouth, Eva thinks, hating that she thinks this. Hating that in some of her memories she and her cousin fucked like gods.

But time has not been kind to him and this pleases her. His fucking mouth is snaggle-toothed. His skull appears spectral beneath his buzz cut. Face gaunt and marked by a small crucifix tat near his left fish eye. Teardrop tat near his right.

She would like to out-stare him. But the guard in the corner nearest Eva yawns and scratches his knee and the clock on the wall is fast. When she dares flick her eyes back to her cousin, he seems to get off on this too. Her trying and failing to face him head on.

Who is she? For god's sake. It's hilarious. So funny she feels she is gobbling gravel.

Just kidding, he says with a wink. I know exactly who you are.

Not one, not two, not three but seriously, four fucking women want to marry him. Crazy shit. One wants to carry his baby, like he'd go for that bull pucky. But another woman, and this is fucking choice, wants to livestream her suicide if the lawyer can't get his sentence commuted, but first she'll take out the lawyer and how cool is that? Seriously though, long shot, they just might commute for good behaviour and the other side's fuck ups and for the sake of some lady who loves him best. And guess what?

He thumbs Eva's direction.

Could be you! Yeah sure, I remember. The most beautiful day. You and me. Forever. Got that on my heart. Got you covered, baby.

He pulls his coverall to one side. A heart tat festoons his left breast. An inked banner snakes the design. Duane, it says at the top, Amy at the bottom.

Amy, Eva says.

He thrusts his ass back in his chair and rocks his torso in tight movements.

Yeah, nearly forgot, he whines. She's dead now. Shit.

He claps a hand to his face.

Amy, he wails. Oh my god, Amy.

The guard in the corner stirs enough to cross his arms, does not get up.

Hey Duane, he calls out. Check it.

I've done a bad bad thing, Eva's cousin says, voice suddenly flat.

Then his eyes light up and he laughs.

Bad bad!

He slams the partition with both hands and jumps to his feet.

I am one bad motherfucker, he shouts, arms thrust wide, jubilant.

The guard strides over, speaking into a device clipped to his shoulder.

And don't you fucking forget it, Eva's cousin yells to the sparsely inhabited room, pumping a fist.

Yeah, Duane, another inmate says. Yeah! Tell it.

On the other side of the room, an inmate and his visitor, a cherubic-cheeked woman holding a squirming toddler on her lap, watch for a few seconds as the guard wrestles Eva's cousin's arms behind him, then the couple resume their conversation.

A second guard lumbers from that side of the room. A door opens and a third guard, this one masked and wearing latex gloves, comes through.

Eva's cousin writhes under their grasp.

Don't forget it, he yells. Don't you fucking ever.

# XVIII

## *nothing much happens*

A Klonopin, two Bloody Marys. Seat belt unbuckled, trench unbelted. Eva At Thirty-five Thousand Feet On The Red Eye Home, Age Forty-One. The occasional flash of lightning in the overcast night sky. A star wanders from behind a cloud like a stray firefly winking—no, a satellite in its orbit.

Everything is atmosphere. So far.

She's in a time before other times, sure of it. Things could be worse than this after-scent of petrichor, the grit of salt in her head. Things aren't so bad.

Things might be semi-bad, that she will allow. For jugs of wine she has none. Nor oil or camels. Nor sheaves of golden wheat. Nor lover or loves. Nor, most likely, a soul-crushing job, not anymore.

She heads to the bathroom, scores another drink, searches in her tote for her book and can't find it—must have left it at the hotel. A little turbulence and she straps in. The captain's voice comes on in a note of crackling static like a song in Eva's head. The static, the song—they make their own weather. Like Eva here. In-between. Over and out.

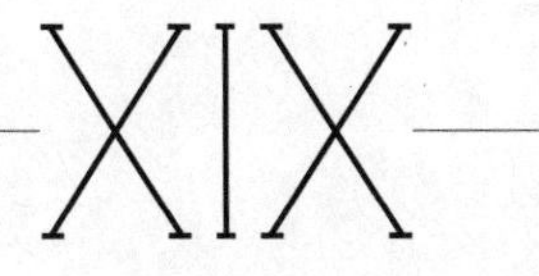

*the shitty weather continues*

She hopes.

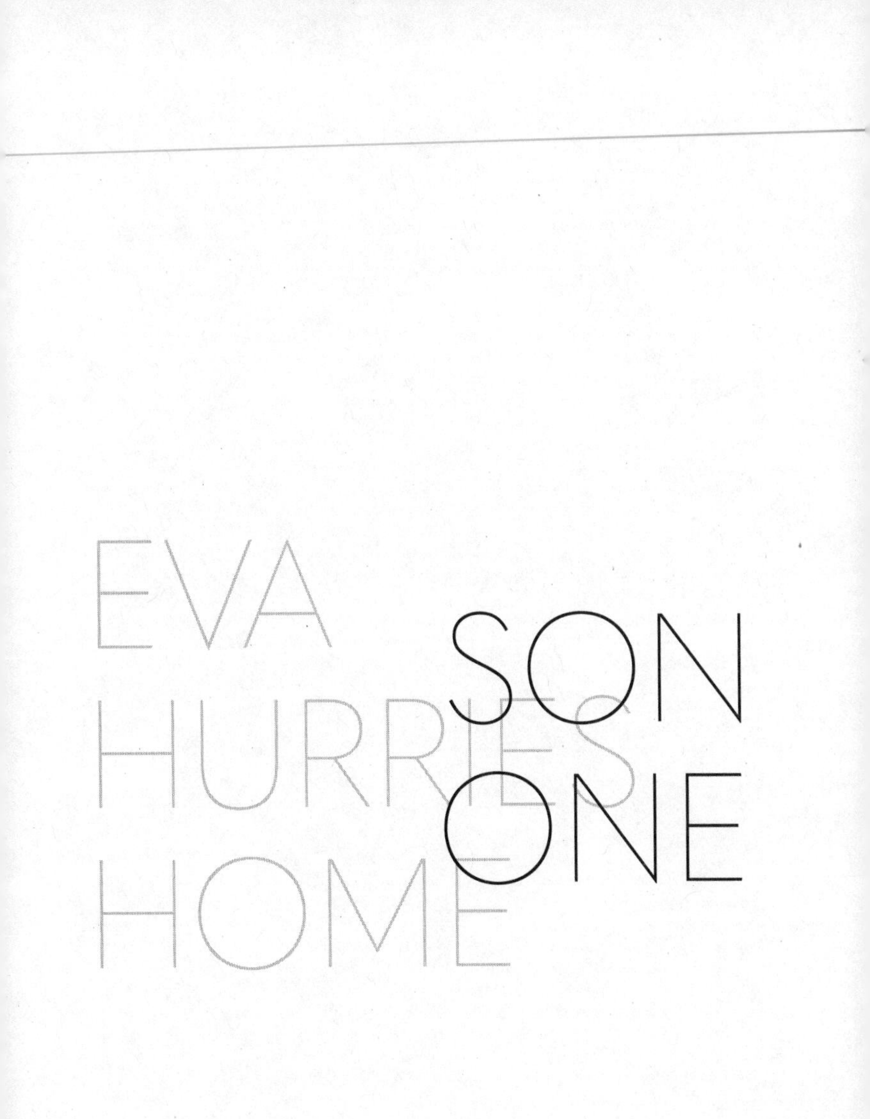
EVA
HURRIES
HOME
SON
ONE

*After the phone call,* our worst fears and suspicions confirmed, I fell for it, as I had fifty years earlier when my mother died: I went to the fridge and opened the door, as if a glass of milk would help.

At that point, May 6, 2005, everything was aftermath.

*Cretins.*

*Dear Adrian:*

Dear Adrian: wait:

Dear Adrian, wait up, it's your sister, can you hear me,
I never took you for so fucking dumb.

Don't be a stranger, danger, you used to say.

*Entered into evidence:* a computer, Adrian's.

Entered into evidence: bloodstains in Adrian's car, in the backseat, the trunk, fingerprints of both accused (stupid, my god), bloodstains on the rug in which they rolled him, rug abandoned in the woods near the tree where they tied him still alive or nearly dead or already dead, entered into evidence photos from the squalid one-bedroom apartment where they first took him, dirty dishes in the kitchen sink, mattress on the floor of the main room, window overlooking a brick wall, blood spatter on everything, the TV, bathroom sink, toilet.

Entered into evidence: Adrian's evident stupidity, I couldn't stop myself from calling it that.

Entered into evidence: records of six ATM transactions on the night of May 4, 2005, using Adrian's card and PIN.

Entered into evidence: records on Adrian's hard drive, five chat messages between him and that, that woman, scarcely a human being, the last from her on May 4, 2005, 3:17 a.m., saying Meet Me at the 7-11 on sandy blvd Good-times ha!, imagine, that night he'd gone straight from a parent-teacher conference with Marcela, separate cars, Adrian coming from the office, Marcela from the community centre where she was (still is) a counsellor for the elderly, he told her he had to head back to the office, pick up something he'd forgotten, home soon, it was 7:54 p.m., the last she saw him, imagine what she had to go through, on top of everything, knowing that.

Everything has already happened, I told Jim in the morning before we left for the Columbus airport and flew to Portland for the arraignment, I couldn't help saying it, It's happened, the worst is over, imagine me the second wife saying this to my second husband at this point in our lives, mid-sixties for me and late seventies for him, but I wanted so badly to hopscotch us past the brutal fact, a father loses his son and in this way, It's over, I told Jim at our layover in Chicago, I couldn't help it, and the look he gave me then, maybe that was the worst.

Evidence: nothing about it made (makes) sense.

*Forget I was the dad* who called him fat-headed on garbage nights for leaving the lid off the pail so the raccoons could feast, full of himself when I complained, forget the year he blasts his metal at all hours and I shout myself hoarse, It's not even music, I yell, and then he fails grade nine biology and goes to summer school, for god's sake the moping, forget the years he fights his kid brother who adores him and over nothing but a borrowed golf tee or a lost comic and forgives in a heartbeat his little sister who idolizes him even when she quote unquote borrows the cologne his first or fifth girlfriend gives him, kid sister with her asthma attacks and hospitalizations and pale clammy skin who takes a stand and dumps said cologne down the toilet, a chip off his block and not mine, unforgettable how at sixteen one night coming home from watching B-ball with some pals he fights off some mugger with our next-door neighbour's purse in his fist and chases this guy for blocks and finally tackles him up some alley and shouts for help until the cops arrive, and hours later, after old neighbourly Mrs. Fisk calls him a hero and the cops pat him on the back in front of me at the station, after we get in the car and I say, Do not tell Lenore-May, you understand? forget that's when he asks me, Dad, what if the guy'd had a gun? and for certain forget I say, Gun? for fuck's sake, Adrian, what if you had a brain?

*Gail, okay, the woman's name,* I repeat it to myself, try to comprehend, human, must be, and though I can't for the life of me do it with the other, the male, at the arraignment I force myself to look at her, scrawny and scuffed-looking when she enters the courtroom, slumps beside the defense counsel, totters to her feet at the all-rise and slumps again, I stare at her matchstick back, rat hair, and all I can think is, Gail?

Goat in my throat at the arraignment and later the first weeks of trial, which turn to months, years I remain glued to this bench in the front row like a fuckwit.

Go on, Lenore-May said to me after the first day in court, the last she and Dad would attend, this was after we'd returned to the hotel, to their suite, Dad helpfully locked in the bathroom with the fan and tap blasting, she put her arms around me, Go on, Michael, she said, cry, let go: one of the things I think about while I wait for recess to end, the word 'recess' reminding me of home, my students in math class, their algebra equations and geometry exercises, calc for the upper levels, and my Sondra, four then five years old, my wife Pam, I'm glad for the break, glad to have this small cry in the bathroom stall on the second floor of the courthouse, the courthouse where I remain, as if in permanent recess from my life before, my life after, the recess before the shit-show starts again.

*In my defense:* I divorced his mother when there was no way around her drinking anymore, I took custody of the kids and, much later, once they grew up some, I married Lenore-May, good on me.

In my defense: I failed as a father a million times over, I must have for him to come to this, if my saying so could bring him back, in my defense.

In my defense, I make a list: Adrian's best friend Sandy who bunked with us when his parents went through a nightmare divorce, Adrian's cat Tigger, dog Lambchop, electric guitar a sixteenth-birthday gift, in my defense though my god it was bloody loud and yes sometimes I yelled about it, in my defense the snub-nosed rat snake Anjelica, in my defense science enrichment after school until he blew all that his grade nine year, in defense hiking trips to Joshua Tree and Shenandoah and Arches, was I not generous to a fault, kidding, for example I was hidebound about law school, insistent and in my defense, shockingly, he listened though what did he do but pass the bar and plow straight into labour law, a rough trade, I warned him, thought at first that's why he'd gone missing, three days later thought it when I learned he'd been killed, thinking he'd landed on the wrong side of some union or union buster, and boy oh my boy, in my defense, was I wrong, guilty as charged.

*I made a list* after the initial calls: what we'd need, a change of sweater and underwear for each of us, a suit and tie for Jim who would refuse to wear them, It's Portland, he said, a simple dress for me, my dead mother's pearls, I'd never before worn them, and I understood then for what and who I'd been saving them.

I thought of who to contact besides the obvious, we'd already spoken daily times who knows with Marcela, my god that poor woman but so strong, and what choice did she have? and sweet Mateo and Daniel, missing their dad and not understanding, like me, missing their dad, getting it and not, I thought we should get in touch with Adrian's old best friend from high school, what was his name? his name and that of his old teacher from grade school he visited that once at the retirement home in Toledo, I thought we might reach out to the aunts on his dead mom's side, I thought of everyone I could, however improbable, and still it wasn't enough to bring him back, and as I thought I fingered my mom's pearls, light grey, I'd heard they change colour adjusting to one's skin, the chemicals or something in the body, alterations of light, scent, who knows? knows how memories are shelved and retrieved, fanciful I know, wasting time when the funeral at that point would be in two days, we had plane tickets to book, a car rental, hotel, needed to pick up Jim's blood pressure pills, at the airport we picked up what

we'd forgotten, ordinaries like toothbrushes and Advil,
I thought up sleep masks, earplugs, extra bottled water,
thought it best to forgo gifts for the boys and Marcela
which ordinarily we'd bring on a trip out to visit, and
I feel bad about it now but I couldn't understand how
I wanted to forget everything, just finger my mother's
pearls in a darkening room, part of me still wants to and
I'm not sure I understand, despite knowing what I now
know about people, some people, my god.

## MICHAEL

*I make lists all day long* and half the night, thinking stuff up, it helps pass the time in the courtroom, better than the time I spend squirming all night on the stiff mattress in my motel room, but can anything really help? help recover what's lost, but here goes anyway: a leech wriggling into his thumb when we were kids fishing at Lenore-May's dad's camp, a sci-fi novel dog-eared and read how many times before finding its way into my hands and read how many more times, a score card we uncharacteristically shared at a Sox game at old Comiskey when we visited Mom's sister in Chicago, and our own sister, her attention shared unevenly, far more interested in her oldest brother and not me the younger, not me the middle child, something else he won at, we also shared a mom who drank, mom who died, we loved to hate her and that's how much I think now we loved her, she meant that much, I know it sounds weird, how intolerable we were, assholes, and then his new family, with Marcela, my new family, with Pam, a mind of my own finally but only sometimes, unwisely asking his big-brother advice on the mortgage, on drawing up a will, the latter a joke in retrospect and a shitty one at that, to this list I add my stubborn ass on this hard bench, day in and out, years pass, I am rooted, mired, stuck in these wrecking conversations I keep having with him in my mind: I say, I am with you, Adrian, while I mull over the plea bargain that allowed your body to be recovered, while I await the verdict, the sentencing, Adrian, I list my love, the crickets we tried to imitate at night when we were little-little, me at fourteen asking your girlfriend to the prom and her shrieks of laughter, me making your famous hash brownie recipe when I was fifteen and still at home and you'd already booted out of there for college and I let it burn to crap, thank god Dad and Lenore-May were away at a conference that weekend, and I called you, Adrian, first born, and you laughed your ass off, you bastard, you dumb fuck how could you be so stupid, I'm on this bench, I know I'm out of order here but nothing I list makes a difference to the outcome, though I can't help but laugh now too, tears down my cheeks: all this crap from a to z an alphabet that creaks and rearranges its atoms, slinks backwards, I hit rewind again, to a time that, some other time that: I don't know, I guess I love you is all I mean, am I making sense?

*I make a list but nothing adds up.*

I make a list but it does nothing to quiet the nineteen minds I hold on the matter, I check it twice, make another and check it three, four, seven times, once for each year since his death.

I make a list: lists: alphabetize, it helps to organize the mind, helps it recover itself, gone full-blown abecedarian I reread the Gnostic gospels from the third century CE, not really my thing, though if they can help why not, from my desk recite them to my office window, a habit I've made of declaiming, helps expand my lungs, no asthma attacks since I was twenty-three, I recite and then restart my own alphabeticals, begin and end with Adrian and these seven, six, five, four years, three, two, one, from my desk add and subtract to make time go and go away, practice circular breathing, also good for the old childhood asthma, should it recur, then force myself to focus on my latest article, invoke Aristotle and Nagel, the private and the public good, I wait for the knock on my door, my student this, student that wanting help with a paper, grade, what can I give them, what lousy partial understanding when my mind plays tricks waiting for the knock that can never come, wait thinking thoughts that lace through my chair, into the floor, down three flights and into the basement, root through the building's foundations and seek deep soil, occulting thoughts despite my reasoning, my seasoned trained mind, joint appointment to Classics and Philosophy, tenured, could have fooled these thoughts like underground streams carving a cavern's shaky air, stalactites that twist through rock rooms and corridors and turn on themselves, while the bazaars of students swirl above, my esteemed colleagues clutch their Ovid and Aeschylus and Engels while, stationed at my desk, I wait for the knock that won't come, wait as if with infinite patience, a joke, I fool everyone but good, especially myself, for the public good I'm no longer sure I believe in, while down below I face endless stone doors, stone corridors, breathe a trapped and dangerous beast's stale breath, my own.

MICHAEL

*June 2004:* add this to the list, the time when Adrian and Marcela and the boys came out to Boulder, late June, last year, a year before this courtroom drama, school was out, Pam and I and little Sondra never had such a good time, it's what we all said, heartily, hitting the day trails all of us together, cooking, chowing, snorting back the wine and beer, smoking some weed while the kids chased fireflies.

June 2004: the last I saw my brother, nothing so fancy as him in silhouette against the sunset or catching my eye and waving one last time when I dropped them all off at the airport, nothing out of the ordinary, nothing memorable, I can't remember that last look and it fucking kills me.

*Knowing what I now know:*

Knowing what:

Knowing you can never really know a person, their slow dissolve leading to a fast end, like a movie screen gone black like that, not just Adrian I'm thinking about, wondering if he'd taken up terrible habits that accumulated over time, or was it a one-off sex chat that escalated, not only that but my mother for instance: years of high blood pressure then dead of a massive stroke days before my fourteenth birthday and then there's Dad: the night after my mother's funeral I turned off the downstairs house lights one by one, overhead in the kitchen, dining room, lamp in the living room to the right of the couch, lamp to the left of the couch, Dad, I said, he was sitting in his chair on the other side of the room, his lamp still on, Dad, I said again when he continued to stare at the floor, I said, Time to go to bed, Dad, want me to get the light for you? and still not looking up he said, For Christ's sake, Lenore-May, are you going to tell me what to do just like your mother did? and knowing ever since then that you can never really know a person, I'm thinking of Jim too: his years of fastidious research into prolonging human life, years of careful eating and where did that get him? and I'm remembering I also learned young, and I told my friend Donna this last night over gnocchi and a half bottle of red: you can't live the rest of your life missing someone who's not there.

## LAURYN

*Lately I'm trying to think again* about the piece of human refuse, sorry, not fair, of course he's human, like everybody else deserving respect and understanding but debased by life and circumstances surely, I get it, try to, thinking how he, and she too, both of them, who can say who led who? anyway thinking how the guy got life in prison, no possibility of parole, the deal struck for the bastard, sorry-not, instead of execution by the state, he led investigators to the body in the woods, the body a not-Adrian, false positive, anyway it's over and I can't forgive, I fail myself with what I want to understand as falsehoods, believe the body false and the body politic broken despite my Aristotle and Voltaire, my books, tenure, students I used to mostly adore, their lives unblighted unlike mine, though what do I know? of my students, of anyone including myself, Adrian: lately I'm like the wolf spider on my windowsill with her eight eyes, except seven of mine are now blind, I see only you and only in outline, in my beam-light this idea of a beloved brother, son, family man, your lawyering on behalf of workers, fairness, justice for all and anger at the state's iniquities, all that like a false positive now, the real you, Adrian I never recognized, never warned, failed as oracle, soothsayer, you, Adrian blinded into dreaming a cold empyreal sleep and where am I going with this, stop.

Lauryn, Dad said when we met in Portland for the arraignment, last time we were all together, Lauryn, it's all up to you now, and these seven years later I still can't for the life of me figure out what he meant, something about my being the most rational one? so rational that I feared asking him and now Dad's gone too, not gone-gone like Adrian but near-gone, thank god for Lenore-May, strong as can be, taking such good care of him, visiting hospice every day since the stroke.

Lauryn, Mike said a few weeks ago on the phone, the terrible-versary, seven solid years now, he said, Do you think we'll ever recover? but who he meant was himself, his pain, how he carried on for all to see and with me, at least, still does, as if he's still there every day in that godforsaken courtroom, I can't forget that about Brother Mike who's doing well enough for himself that he made principal at his high school two years ago, good for him, I can't begrudge him some success, a little happiness, though I do envy him, my own pain and shame and anger, and fear too, especially fear, of brokenness and stranger danger when I lock up my office at night and slouch to my car in the near-empty lot, fear in the middle of the night when I hear my apartment settle, Who's there? I call out, and fear of my own murder mind when I think of those monsters, fear of how easily I demonize despite my thinking on justice, I degrade their humanity as they did Adrian's and so am no better, in a way, a conceptual way, in so doing I debase my own humanity, step beside myself, become another Lauryn, Lauryn driven deep and sleepless, desiring retribution, mouth a silent cave of white spiders, their seven of eight eyes blind, eyes milky and pale, pale and clammy as my skin when I used to have my asthma attacks when I was a kid and thought I was breathing my last, Lauryn, stop, stop thinking this, where was I?

Lilac time: outside my office window it's May again.

Lilac time restore me, after all is said and done train me to again recognize tree, tree, shrub, purple and pale pink, gaggle of students, here's one now with a knock on my door, no more time for this in-between time, it's my office hour, I have a job to do, thank god I have my job to do.

*Little gestures,* I tell myself after my student leaves, take time for the little things like the kindness of tulip and forsythia in a vase on my filing cabinet, snort of bourbon from the bottle in my desk drawer, time for you, Adrian, now that my student has left and I'm here alone hands splayed on my desk so they feel full: I trace the half moons on my fingernails as I once traced yours, begged you to let me do it, here is where I'll stay in this time between time, hand to hand with you, a bear of a big brother, my six-year-old's hamsa for you, my innocent gift at the time gains an oracular dimension or is that overstating? overblown for your protection, I would hyperbolize anything, drop my critical stance, to keep you safe, if I could, as if.

Lunulae, those fingernail half moons are called, as were the amulets young girls in ancient Rome sported around their necks, pendants in the shape of a crescent moon to ward off evil forces and protect against the evil eye: if they could protect me now from myself, I'd: I'd: I have no belief: including in myself, self comprised of all I know including the so little I knew growing up, little stupid me lapping up all praise and thinking I could protect myself with prizes, with Columbia and Oxford and Stanford like amulets around my stiff neck, little did I know you, Adrian, or that you were the one needing protection, so little did I know you and it kills me.

## MICHAEL

*Michael needs to get a grip,* Dad said to Lauryn, this was yesterday, after day one of the trial, prosecution evidence and witnesses, she's sitting in the front seat of the rental after he's picked us up from the courthouse, as if I, seated in the backseat blowing my fucking nose, can't hear him, and who the crap is he to talk, bug-eyed blue-veined bald head, this old man who's just decided he can't bring himself to attend the courtroom sessions, Lenore-May has to baby him in their suite, take him for walks in the park for fuck's sake, I mean seriously, they should've stayed in Columbus, left me in this courtroom with Lauryn, though she'll tire soon I'm guessing, decide to stay in Boston, I have my students to think of, I bet she'll say, my department, and I'll say, What about me and my students? and she'll say, That's your choice, she'll abandon me here on this bench to the lawyers and judge and jury, onlookers and reporters, fistful of true-crime ghouls who keep trying to interview me, keep calling and emailing me, Dad and Lauryn too and how did the creeps figure out our numbers and email addresses? anyway Lauryn leaving me too, alone with my inability to understand Adrian truly dead, how can I comprehend when I feel his lips at the back of my neck breathing hard AF, like those times he wrestled me down when were kids and he won, he won, he won.

Mike needs to get a grip, Lauryn announced, this was yesterday, we'd arrived back at the hotel, Lenore-May left Dad alone in the bathroom and ignored Lauryn's pronouncement, Lenore-May, god I do love her, she led me to the sofa, sat me down next to her, said, You're doing fine, Michael, given the circumstances, thank you for being so brave, and it's not that I feel brave or need praise but thank fucking god for Lenore-May.

Mikey, get a grip, for god's sake, I imagine Adrian saying to me here in court, day two of the trial, wouldn't you know it Lauryn's already gone and taken a pass, didn't lose much time, I called that one, Mikey, Adrian says, lips grazing the back of my neck like we're wrestling again, Quit it, I tell him silently, I'm tired! I don't bother saying my spine kinks, gut twists, My butt's sore! I'd like to tell him from this goddamn bench, but his breath's on me, I can't stop my feeling of dumb relief, of course I lose, all my life he's been better at everything, but I don't turn around, head up, chin up, pretending he's not there, pretending not to feel this shame at what he did, inviting disaster, the reckless fuck, I can't believe he did that and I'm pretending not to anticipate anyone who might regard what role he played in his own murder as shameful, his murder shameful, all murder unnatural-seeming, nothing innocent about it, those of us even vaguely touched by the Biblical tradition of Cain and Abel, not really my jam as my school kids might say but what a story, brother against brother, the horror of that, all bonds off, in my pretending I fantasize I get up in their judgmental faces, shout a fuck you at every man woman child unmurdered, crazy I know but I can't help it, the lucky fucks, how do they rate? seriously, listen to me! pretending it's not and will not always be May 5, 2005 in my head: the night or following day that you, Adrian, you got yourself killed: and it's not me with you in your terrible moments, holding your head, beaten, my hands on your chest, beaten, tugging your shoeless big toes, a detail from court, the animals stole your shoes, your shoes! but I'm here for you now no matter what, your breath on my neck, in my ear, I'm ready to face the shame and anger and cry like a jerk, witness evidence and witnesses, the sad pageant continues, all rise for Her Honour and I do, laser my eyes like hot hell on the back of this fucker's neck, he is alive and breathing on the other side of the bar from me and if I could stop his breath with my mind I would.

*Non-starter,* no go, never will such language cross my lips, even if I could move my lips, could speak, moan, cry out, not in a million would I ever say it.

Now, however, a one-time only offer, what the damned stroke has gifted me: besides the reprehensible greatest hits of on-hold music playing every damn day at the nurse's station, don't think I can't hear the gifts of time travel, high-flown fancy thinking when I'm able to think at all, my first-born a baby in nebulae of asters on a summer trip to Idaho to see my mom and dad, my wife not yet a full-on drunk, she wavers sunlit at the edge of the field calling, Baby look, baby see, she laughs at me fiddling with my camera, used to call me the fiddler on the campus at Ohio State, me with my learned papers, my research, my low-carcinogenic diets for the sake of long life, sake of trying to beat the old family curse of high blood pressure and high incidence of major stroke, You goddamned fiddler arounder, she called me when drunk, a full-on drunk in time, the kids ten and seven and five when I divorced her, at least she cut the booze when pregnant, I give her that, crazy dead soul, anyway I divorced her and that ended that.

Now I piece more together: first Lenore-May's old dog Layla had a stroke by my side of the bed, poor girl, she lay like that all of Sunday two years ago, and on Monday the vet recommended by our vet came over, did the merciful deed, and who will do such for me? when I know Lenore-May would never, The worst is over, she'd say if I could ask, but how would she know? how measure her knowing against what I know, that I didn't beat anything did I, beaten into a hospice bed, Lenore-May bless her visits daily, feeds me slice after slice of mango, pear, my favourites, can't turn my head to see so can only imagine her lovely and smart at seventy-one and not immune to flattery from the doctor who tells her he doesn't know how much if anything I comprehend, including how lucky I am to be hand-fed mango and pear by such a beautiful lady, now: now: where was I? gone and lost my train of thought, there was a funeral once, I've forgotten whose, okay semi-forgotten, city streets blocked off for miles, where, rain for days, Will you look at that, I said to Lenore-May, I said, It's like he was some hero or something and maybe he was and I never knew it, or I did but forgot, and she said, I know, I know.

*On the first anniversary* of Jim's death, eight and change since Adrian's, sixty since Mom's: my friend Donna and I get to the airport early and caffeinate and people-watch and when we land first thing we hop over to the Guggenheim for the Brancusi-Serra show, marvellous, we check into our hotel in midtown, an early dinner at the most wonderful trattoria, reminds me of the time Jim and I and Adrian and Marcela and the boys, very young, went to Venice and ordered a huge platter of squid in ink and: and: anyway it's the next morning, Donna and I take the subway to Prospect Park, stop at an artisanal perfumery recommended online, try scent after scent, drive the guy behind the counter nuts and later take an architecture tour by boat from near Battery Park, I tell Donna I feel sad and free and she squeezes my hand, all the feels, as the kids say, Adrian and Marcela's adopted Mateo and Daniel and Michael and Pam's Sondra, I miss them, so before dinner at the fancy Indian place we FaceTime in two separate calls, a miracle I catch them, dinner's amazing, my god the raita ice cream! and I don't feel guilty for one second, now it's the next afternoon and we're at our gate people-watching, all that motion and emotion and everything hits me, I do feel guilty and Donna says, Are you okay? and I say, No, yes, who knows?

*Question: How long in this room?*

Question: is it noon when the light blinks through the blind or half past three?

Questions: if I have no arms or legs why a mouth? a mouth so Lenore-May can stoop to kiss me each day as if I deserve it, stuff me with sliced mango and pear? and if my mind shifts, time-infected, and I see her dog panting on her side and the wide-eyed fear, is that this or another now?

# MICHAEL

*Right away I feel it,* another day in court, Adrian's secret breath smoky and tart at my neck, and this time I'm so relieved I nearly piss myself.

*Shifting sands,* tides that turn, can't trust what you love: I can't escape the clichés, the plane takes off and slow-loops over the ocean, rivers, I recall Jim's old nonsensical joke about his Number One Son turning to Son One and add in Son Two they don't add up to much of anything, a thing he'd say when they were teens and he'd be good and mad at them, good kids but Jim had little patience then, the boys ciphers both, I often couldn't catch their drift or Jim's at times, to be honest, it's like they spoke their own private language, idioglossia I think it's called? whatever it's called, and now can't catch my own drift, first time for everything I suppose but I don't care, it's my age, I expect, a justification I'm eager to grasp, such is life, I think, another anodyne attempt and I tighten my seatbelt and Donna pats my knee, okay, we're okay, I think of Son Two, easily graspable compared to his older brother, poor Michael now principal of the high school where he taught math all these years, a good man, sensitive, since his brother died medicated to a high level of functionality, is what he jokes, that he can joke a miracle when I think of all that's happened, which I sometimes forget, given the crisis with Jim's stroke, I dropped and forgot so much: my volunteering at the community arts centre, my plan to go with Donna to the shelter and each pick out a dog, I'll email the centre when we get back, see if they need help again, look into the dog situation, and of all things I sometimes forget or is it forgive: Son One, burly, mentally tenacious like his dad and sister, successful lawyer, father, husband, until he wasn't, and how much does that one instance matter beyond the obvious, that it killed him? can't we just weigh all the good against the one bad, the big bad, can't I try to stop thinking in terms of these absolutes, recall my mother saying when I was little, There's good and bad in everyone, can I stop overthinking when even these years later the raw shock shakes me and my throat closes, good, bad, if they don't matter then nothing does, I hate thinking like this but can't help it.

*Stranger danger:* I keep returning to it and hating myself for it, Adrian, but Adrian, if you'd only had a brain, you could've thought that one through on your own.

*Under over* on how many students will ask for an extension on their final paper?

Until we meet again, that's the joke in our department at the end of every lame-o meeting, I should write a book, Goofs I Have Known, present self included.

Usually I wait until after my nine o'clock class to suck down some fine bourbon chased with breath mints, but not today, this May day so near the anniversary, not tomorrow either, all hell could break loose, cheers.

*Vroom!* Sondra roars when I phone after court session and ask her how school was today, Vroom? I ask, and kick myself, what kind of a question is that? and, no fool, no time for idiot dad, of course she's gone, my precious girl, I have to remind myself of who and what she is to me while I'm here in this courthouse hallway, and now she's gone, poof, handing the phone back to Mommy.

*Who asks how I am,* Not good, I tell her, Come home, I can't, You mean won't, Not until the trial is over and sentencing is complete, Your girl needs you, we both do, your students need you, I'm so sorry, are you sure you're okay?

Whodunit: irrefutable, also how and why, but still I want the details, the ridiculous pinstripes on the defense counsel's suit, scabby red skin on both defendants' faces, poor posture and jitters from their lives of want for which uncharacteristically I care nothing, me the caring teacher, the nice guy who, like his brother, served the underdog, instead I want the torture of seeing justice done even if it means seeing them daily, want my own suffering to serve as substitute for what he suffered, want to substitute our joint suffering for what I most desire, a brother, this once-boy: despite the gray early May weather, in Ohio the sun trying to come out, fledgling light flashing intermittently on a bridge handrail and our fishing poles bent and vibrating, hooked one! hooked two! our conjoined breath a hideaway, we are safe here and filled with mist, we have swallowed it, nothing can touch us now.

Whodunits: another thing I call them, those accused, I study them further, the nearly indistinguishable heads, both shaggy blond with dark roots showing as if a single beast I refuse to recognize as human, equal parts junk male and female, a shit species distant by galaxies from the brother perfect as any imperfect human can be, who they stole.

Whoever they are, who any of us are, even you, Adrian, brother who fucked up as anyone might, fucked up but was undeserving of death, whoever I am now, this person I no longer recognize whose tears persist, last so long each drop turns to stone.

*Xystus:* a long and open portico used especially by ancient Greeks or Romans, and so in my wheelhouse, for athletic exercises in wintry or stormy weather, it'll do, Adrian, it's me, Lauryn here, still playing my alphabet game, organizing, sorting the unsortable, up to STUVX now, frivolous though it might be can you tell me, am I winning?

Xystus, sometimes: a walk lined with trees, I like this one better, the better to stroll along in moody mental weather and attempt to find the beauty in mourning or at least believe it might exist, an aesthetics of loss at which I scoff even as I yearn for it, and where was I? I was here, walking with you in my head, forgive me this indulgence, would you?

JIM

*You want to know how it happened?* and you want to know the why? and well good luck with that.

You want to know what I'm thinking, lying here with nothing to do on my lucid days but think about how I can't compliment or grouse at Lenore-May about the nurses or ask her to play me the Shostakovitch String Quartet #5 off her phone, the Brodsky Quartet recording from 1989, released on Teldec, or say to her, Was it a cloudless day? a day when maybe he looked back at his screen, clicked away and back again, Hello can you help me my name is Gail you don't know me but I hear you are a man of your Word.

You want to know more? more of was he and was he not? well forget it, it doesn't matter, what does count is that he was human and I want more now, my body brain dwindling, want final details, what I couldn't bear to know right after it happened, and now, now I want all I can get, I do, don't, do.

# MICHAEL

*You can't trust what you love.*

*Zeno of Elea:* Of course you'd come up with that, Lauryn, Adrian would say, he'd say, Why the fuck not Zenith? but Zenith calls to mind Nadir, too sad to think about, which is why I'll go with the old Greek instead, so bear with me, Adrian, for the way is arduous, a rough ride, but can't one hope to find hope?

Zeno: whom (bear with me while I get up on my hind legs and talk the talk!) Aristotle called the inventor of dialectic and who, according to Diogenes Laertius in his *Lives and Opinions of Eminent Philosophers*, written in Greek in the first half of the third century CE, "could argue both sides of any question" (trans. mine) and as I argue in my latest article, accepted I found out yesterday by email for the *Proceedings of the Aristotelian Society*, influenced Aristotle's *Physics*, Zeno's paradoxes being arguments against motion and moving forward and tidy endings, to which you can bet I can relate! and also allow me to note the apocryphal stories of Zeno resisting to his death various tyrants including Demylus, whose tongue Zeno bit off and "spit it in the tyrant's face" (trans. mine), and look I know this is all very tortuous, but following wise Zeno I bite my tongue in order to resist motion and endings, those autocrats, certain the only thing stirring is me, working fastidiously like Zeno to argue both sides, entertain the possibility of reformation if not forgiveness and, politely though noncommittally, field calls from the anti-deathers, while the pro-deathers reach out to me and I think, oh yeah, yes yes yes, and wait in my office for my student, and in my waiting I stare at the online reproduction of the fresco *Zeno Shows the Doors to Truth and Falsity* from the sixteenth century CE, now in the collection of the Library of El Escorial, Madrid and in this way I keep the beast at bay, brother dead, father nearly dead, a zenith of sorts, I suppose Adrian would be right, a rest stop, resting place, no better and no worse, dead zone dead zone dead.

*You'd think the world had come to an end,* first with Adrian, now with each slice of mango or pear that might be my last, and all I can think, and I wish I could tell Lenore-May this: I don't believe but if I did I'd say, Whoever you are up there, you got me good, joke's on me.

*You can't trust what you love.*

*X marks the spot?* I wonder, right now over these clouds on the way back to Columbus, or would that be too callous of me? to call it now, the end, time to move on, can I trust myself to know the right time?

*Whosoever:*

Whosoever: though I don't believe, whosoever let me return to my wife and daughter and school kids, justice served, whatever that means, end my brother's death, and mine, rot-rooted to this bench.

With practise I'll return home even when home, watch Sondra dig worms in the yard and chatter to them in her private language, put her down for a nap, observe her restless dreaming seemingly intricate as the spirals of her ear canals, is that where she goes, in and around and wakes flapping her little hands, digs her tiny fingernails into her eye sockets, the official diagnosis autism, Pam and I tape socks onto her hands, daily, nightly and Pam earns her PhD in special ed and I grade algebra tests and learn the hard ways to finally say, Remember back then? I'm so glad it's over, where the heck even was I?

*Whenever I think:*

Whenever I think we're in the dark cellar, hidden away and near the end, I wonder what "we" I'm thinking of: me, we, these circles I make in my mind, my mind having nothing else to do, no other place to go but in these circles.

Whenever I think my condition worsens: whenever I think, my condition worsens.

*Worse than the worst* of my students, I search for the teachable in all this and can't, just can't, and what is the lesson if not learned?

We tried, Michael and Dad and Lenore-May, each of us in our own way, I believe that but:

We buried no one we knew.

We are in a time before other times, I try to believe that, I do.

*Well it's been a day,* a couple of days, and when I give in and cry on the plane's approach to Columbus, these loops above cornfield and forest, Donna leans over and pats my knee, Honey, she says, what a time you've had: as if I could ever be over things.

*Venting again,* and does the distraction ever feel good: videoconferences are the worst, at least Adrian and Dad never had to deal with them, that's what crazy drunk Mom would have called a blessing, bless her, and where did that come from? my heart dry as dust the after-second I think it, thinking of my own mother! and is that why Adrian had to die? so I could become human, semi-human, if only for an instant, so in this way am I not like that, what to call her, thing, monster, that woman? am I not something like her?

*Us:*

Us all.

Until we meet again, under the old oak tree? with me buried under with these chirpy tunes from the nurses' station, until these ridiculous ear-worms cease and desist, they're driving me nuts, burrowing around and around my ear canals, worming those labyrinths, I've enough of a brain left for that, oh joy, kill me now.

Ultrasound time again, whoopee, the nice lady waves her wand over my belly which of course I can't lift my head to see and there's no way to ask, and later, same day? following week? and what the hell is a day or week now anyway, anyway later I hear Lenore-May on her phone, worried, What's it matter, I want to say, the worst is most unconscionably over, remember, honey, the worst being over? which would be the worst thing I could possibly say and a good thing I can't, she'd be no-joke mad.

(*Understand there's no one* to text or email or call about any of this, maybe Lenore-May but she's been through so much I don't want to further impose, maybe Mike but he has Sondra to take appointment to appointment and his school to run now that he's principal and Pam now with her chemo, my god it never ends, he's told me he makes dinner for them, a nice pasta, I imagine, a simple salad, glass of wine if Pam's up to it, so I'll just go ahead thinking on my own here.)

Under the old oak in Dad's backyard in Columbus, brightness drifts down, I'm just back from the hospital, asthma again, and I know in my good-girl bones how lucky I am, brothers sprawled on their stomachs near me working a crossword together, unusual and sweet their togetherness, sweet the clumps of grass I pull cool in my hand.

Under the arcade in Padua two spring breaks ago, rain streams past the colonnade, somewhere a bell chimes, I gasp for breath, asthma? which I outgrew, and now how old I am, feeling like I'm walking for five years ten years on your death day, Adrian, feeling myself dead and calling to you alive in a dimension I can't hear, since then I carry my inhaler with me everywhere, which is increasingly not far, desk to window, window to desk.

*Those jackals, they were the worst,* that's what I'd like to discuss again with Lenore-May, okay not quite the worst, but close: the journalists, I know that sounds flippant or right-wing or something, and I do get it, the importance of the press, reporting the truth, bearing witness, believe me I've never been one of those people, but the ways in which the animals descended when the news first broke, local TV, local print, their questions on the courthouse steps following the arraignment, nearly the same as what Mikey would go through every day during the trial, sentencing, verdict, Can you comment on your son's emails, his chat messages, the plea bargain struck with the state, and the five years that passed after the fact when I was still of sound mind and body, that's when the worst of the worst crawled out of woodwork, Can I interview you for my book about the criminal mind, mental illness, my book that's a riveting, visceral blur of reportage and autobiography, a mystery to be solved in the course of reading, a deep dive into the mystery of a drug addict, a killer, his unwitting or semi-witting victims including his girlfriend, your son, you as a survivor, surviving what? I want to know, can anyone tell me that?, these proposed books about someone not my son dragged into the dark nexus of sex and murder, these so called-writers, blood-sucking shits wanting their grief served hot and if I could forget I would, of all things my ruined body and mind won't let go of their emails and microphones and camera-smiles, they swarm me at night when Lenore-May's returned home, the nightmare aftermath miniaturized, they crawl across the ceiling of this godforsaken room and flit down to sting my ears, bite my throat, these after-the-fact assassins, I can't stop my mind from running on, if I could kill my mind I would, rip the uselessly turning wheels churning this sack of shit body that used to be me.

*This flight never seems to end.*

Thinking for no reason of the time Jim stopped by the information desk at the library and asked me out for coffee, he was an associate dean, as my boss's boss he shouldn't have asked me, but those were different times, thinking too of before that time when I divorced my first husband and, not much later, an in-between time, earned my master's in library science.

The time I ran a 5k for the Heart and Stroke Foundation, ironic now, crossing the finish line I heard some man yell, Look at the flamingo legs go! and Jim yelled, That's no bird, that's my wife, jerk! and another time I'm thinking of, no particular rhyme or reason, when Jim and I took the boys and Lauryn to Zion for March break, Jim and the kids up there on the arch so close to the damn edge and I'm beside myself on the ground, clamping my hands down over my eyes, heart in my mouth, for god's sake Jim, what are you thinking, I'm thinking, until I can't take it any longer, head back to the car, fish the extra set of keys from my daypack, spend a good hour locked inside cooling and heating and cooling before they saunter back laughing, at me I think, until I unlock the doors and Jim's busting a gut so hard he can hardly get out that he'd placed them under direct orders not to fall or else I'd kill him, my god, time of small jokes, unfunny jokes, small and private pleasures, mixed pleasures, small and private pains, what I wouldn't give.

The redbud in Dad's backyard in St. Louis, where I grew up.

The earthworm casings in the vegetable-garden soil fascinated me when I was five, everything intriguing and new, like the scent of the ripe cherries I at fourteen undertook to pit for a pie, for Dad, Mom too sick from the chemo to bake let alone eat, fascinating even the sickening sense, in a finger-stained moment, of my own stupid attempts to fill in for her as I rolled out dough for a crust for the first and last time in my life.

The blue swing.

The alder.

That day Dad and I buried Mom.

*To my wife:* kindly forgive my complaints about the humidity-headache courtroom lights.

To my daughter: forget-me-not while I'm away, even when I'm home.

To my brother: you were first, nothing could ever change that, nothing could change me, second son, middle child, not up to the task of rising to take your place, Your Honour, only up to this, my sore ass on a hard bench while I think backward to three minutes ago when the man-perp yawned and I felt it in my own jaw, how sick is that? and even farther back to the chicken wrap I bought for lunch an hour ago, tossed after one bite, cup of coffee at dawn in my hotel room, yesterday's green-striped tie, last week's diarrhea, two years ago your trip to Boulder, Adrian, your Mateo swallows a butterfly, we wonder should we worry, and seventeen years ago your astonishing sideburns and premium asshole way of congratulating me on teacher's college, a resigned slap on the shoulder and half-happy Good on you, bro, and long before that the frog you tried to force me to eat when Lenore-May's dad wasn't looking, and now back again to this bench, it's like everything that ever was unwinds, bro, and I'm benchmated as if in a newly invented chess game, remember how you used to beat me at it every time, check check checkmate, now I am eternally beaten by you, Number One Son, and all that's happened.

The voyeurs in court every day: cameras thrust in my face as I stumble on the sidewalk in front of the courthouse, calls from reporters and true-crimers up and down the west coast and also a handful from Ohio, before whose eyes I weep.

The videoconference with my principal: in which she voices support and I weep before her eyes.

The verdict:

The shame and anger and exhaustion before the verdict and after: I'm out of order here, I know.

The courtroom: 'til death do us part.

The counting of days in court: though I am all out of order, Your Honour, moving backward, forward, listing in my seat, I count but remain undone.

The crying:

The crime:

*The question, the search for an answer.*

The question of rehabilitation, before or after the question of justice.

The question of redemption, question of forgiveness.

The thingness of things versus the abstract, brotherly sweat and hoot-laugh, armpit farts, a brother face-down in the pool, dead-man's float, I was four and scream scream screamed and you lifted your head and howled like a like a like

The brother in space and time and not.

*So much for thinking:* it beggars belief, and speaking of begging:

Say it to me again, I implore you, say anything, even if it's something like goodie-girl Lauryn, go fuck yourself, get a life: as you did when I asked, innocence itself, Is that hash you're baking into those brownies?

Say this: tell me the one about the piece of string walking into a bar, make me howl and pee myself, make me eat the green Play-Doh by telling me I'll grow a second set of ears, tell me they'll be the better with which to hear you, my dear.

Say it: shred the silence in my office, rip my auricles and funnel into my auditory canal and circle down its tunnel, unravel your red thread, the oracle with no sense of timing warning me dead dead you're dead, say the news and I grow horns, I, Asterius the starry one, writ as Taurus in the sky, I wait for you down here, my coarse fur steaming, I sharpen hooves on stone, it's all I hear, my insides turned to stone corridors through which I stamp along the red thread of your leaving us.

Say Euripides had it right: a mingled form and hybrid birth of monstrous shape, my grief over you, trying to be you, your nature both man and bull, you tenderly plucking inchworms from my hair, brute force with which you bullied Mike, say it's me you can't hear, say it, you bastard, my good-girl learning you poked until we spoke rarely and only by phone in your last years, we called on birthdays and hadn't much to say, I made sure to visit Dad only when you weren't there, did you use the same strategy, relieved at my absence? absent the pride we could have taken in each other.

Say: Cut it out, Lauryn, what's all this crap? for crap's sake, Lauryn, you used to be the smart one.

LAURYN

*Say anything?*

JIM

*Ridiculousness all around, stop.*

*Queasy,* I tell Donna when the turbulence starts up, she takes my hand, miracle of a friend that she is.

*Please, God I don't believe in,* please, gods, pretty please make this stop.

*Oracle says:* Save the last dance for me? dance in how far it is from the window to the ground.

Oracle says: Never mind, save it, sister, unleash not your worst furies, your time is nowhere yet near.

Oracle says: Go on! go out for that drink with colleagues, take a load off, sound good? just be sure to bring that inhaler, couldn't hurt.

*No, I will never write a book about it.*

*No, I will never write about it,* some kind of tell-all, but thanks for asking, Adrian, thanks too for being here for me: don't worry, I do know you're not, joke, is all.

*No, I still won't speak to them* and I would never write my own, sorry Donna, yes I agree it might be therapeutic, but nothing's changed, I can live without the circus, though I appreciate the thought.

*Making time:* for a minor study of elegy, for this unripe apricot I couldn't resist buying, eating it quick before my student shows, time for the tercets I dreamed for you last night that dissolved on my morning walk to class, for my trembling at the memory of the time I received the worst news of my life, you dead, dead for all time, time for my shaking now in my office chair and making good time as I streak toward you, trying to, you upside down on the jungle gym though you were already a teen, you racing along the beach in Cape Cod flying a kite, you let me hold the string once, you held my shoulders so I wouldn't lift into the sky, I guarantee it, Lauryn, you promised, I won't let you go, you pushing poor scrawny Mike, all of thirteen years old, onto the floor and pinning him with a knee and forcing his mouth open with one hand and with the other spraying the Reddi-wip in to make him choke, you wiping his tears and apologizing, you saying, Try not to cry all your life over me, the two of you laughing, calling truce, how many truces over time? and in recent years you've ducked behind the fourth section of the Apocalypse Tapestry at Chateau d'Angers and pieced yourself into the mosaic on the triumphal arch and apse semi-dome in the Basilica of Sant'Apollinare in Ravenna, I go often online since I first visited IRL with my ex-husband, the art historian nearly as old as Dad, always you in this time in-between, before my student at the door and my afternoon's grad seminar discussion, Aristotle on the private, on the sphere of moral good, political good, when I'll speak out of my mouth while I make time for your secret words in my ear like some oracle, you saying, Good Lauryn, good-girl Lauryn, don't you know your alphabet project can make only sad sounds?

Make it stranger, I tell myself: make my minor study of elegy more numinous, study gnosis and not just the episteme, the doxa, and maybe also listen when Oracle says, Nice try, Lauryn, but it's just not you.

Making do: my fourth book under contract, *Justice and Redemption in Ancient Thought*, my students and teaching award, hopes for promotion to full professor, my professional pride I hope can save me.

*Keepsakes:* artisanal perfume with floral and citrus notes, more frou-frou than I would have previously gone for, and a slightly torn vintage Pucci silk scarf because Donna said you only live once, which reminded me of moving from St. Louis to Chicago when I finished college at Washington U and I walked the Magnificent Mile every evening after work at the bank, window-shopping, of course I couldn't afford a thing there, instead bought boxes of Frango mints from Fields on State Street, and now I've also got this sore left calf from all the walking Donna and I did this weekend in New York, but we had so much fun I'm not complaining, a small box of Jacques Torres truffles, here, let me reach into my bag under the seat in front of me and snag them, though the stewards have been through the cabin for the final prepare for landing, offer them, saying, Do you think? and Donna says, Go for it, girl, in direct contradiction of the keepsakes of my Missouri upbringing, which are, I'll believe it when I see it, and Don't get too high on yourself, and Find a life you can live and make no excuses for, and Go on and do what you need to do and remember to always thank me, Yours, Dad.

*Jim-Dad,* he called me a few times when he was twenty-five, home for what turned out to be the last time, pre-law, finally, I told him, time to get serious guy, I was worried about all the time he'd wasted after college touring Croatia, Portugal, Israel, a kibbutz! but at least they put him to work, god knows where else, Mongolia for all I cared, with his Yes Jim-Dad this, Yes Jim-Dad that when I only asked him to mow the goddamn lawn, can you believe it? believe I still can't? believe the sneering little shit who just had to goad me over my morning paper, coffee in my yellow mug, my opinions at the dinner table over roast chicken and cuke salad, a modest burgundy, finally I said, Adrian, wait until you're a father, then you'll know: and it's like that, I'm stuck with it and not proud, I always in remembering, when I can remember at all, have the last word, my memory another thing about me that, if I'm honest, has gone all to shit.

*I keep at,* make lists to pass the time, try to sharpen the old shit-box of a brain, think up I-words today, yesterday was J? J or H, but the I-words are the best, remind myself I'm here, I am, I am, I am moving forward for a change, ibuprofen for pain, that's a joke! and Icarus which is no comment, can of worms, and Idiopathic, which I wish, but it's the stroke, stupid.

I forge ahead and backward again: iPod that Lenore-May brought last week to play Bach and Hammerstein, imagining life in this old bastard yet, Ignoble would be about right to describe how I lie here and other things I shall not mention, wait, go back, Imbricate is how I feel, good one! as I'm like imbricated sedimentary edges overlapping and aligned with paleocurrent and glacial, don't I sound like a dictionary now! good on me these mental exercises, might not be improving but at least I'm not utterly dead yet, anyway I'm imbricated, though there's still Lenore-May and her steady white hand, orange fruit, the pale one too, called what? the fruit with the shivery teeth in my throat, clever and secretive all the way down.

*It all starts again, won't quit.*

I tug my tongue and set it wagging for my students' sakes, let them know I'm here, perform hearing them out, hoping this will bring me back, learning from them as I used to aver, but beneath their bright words it's true my private alphabet spells only elegies, spells sad.

I see the only stranger danger is me.

I pull these strands, and strings unravel and curl, red threads bind my wrists, I'm bound to not make sense between students during office hours, between each one, each student, each hour, I wait for the knock on my door, wait for my beast's red eyes to glow, the knock that comes, never who I desire most, the knock comes and I double-speak for the sake of my students, these fair sons and daughters, for their sakes I try to forget my missing, these sons and daughters as if of Thebes, I can't help thinking, seeing I must in time sacrifice my brother for the greater good.

I miss you, miss Dad-who-once-was, Michael-who-once-was, like men in a stupid fairytale, it's the job of my missing to restore them, or, in an alternate version, to reach a point where I miss my missing, a flinty regret, in an after time when I'm free.

In a time between times.

*I miss Pam and Sondra and my students* and the missing yawns wide, swallows me in a way that's the opposite of missing my brother, a relief to miss the living, a problem I can solve.

*I miss them all, but that's no way to live.*

# LAURYN

## *1*

# LENORE-MAY

*1*

LAURYN

*Herodotus!* thank god for you, though your histories of this happened and that happened sometimes bore me out of my mind, but don't worry, when my student comes I won't let on.

*For the life of me,* once this plane finally touches down and we get our ride and I unlock my front door at long last, I don't know what I'll do or how, but I guess I'll figure it out from there.

*Even after sitting three hours straight,* one hour off for so-called lunch, three more hours, even at the final All rise, I stand and imagine it's you rising, your ascent, fuck no I'm still not religious, it's just that, it's just: ah fuck: I can't quit seeing you in my head, I swear it's one badass cannonball in reverse, bro, and for a second you've got me laughing, got me good, not such a terrible way to end.

Eject, okay? and say, It's over, the end, an end, like flipping a cassette, remember those? and starting over, making like I'm not here and never have been and you're not in a permanent somewhere else, the courtroom dissolves, guards gone, judge vanished, jury pissed off on permanent recess, and those two: those two: eject them from the face of the earth, Your Honour, if it pleases you, as I can never forgive, as I secretly wanted the death penalty for both, not that I'd shared that with the execution advocates or agreed to share a whisper with the anti-deathers, but what I needed to say publicly I did in my Victim Impact Statement, a serviceable outline, what the fam feels, a community's loss, and keeping my rage razor tight, quote unquote appropriate and not haphazard and panicked, not at all like the fuckers with their rage loosed, a degraded rage, unconstrained, and their rage over what? what terrible lives they'd lived, abuse and cruelty I could try to imagine but won't, not now, not yet, not ever, if those fuckeries ever come up for parole they can be sure I'll be there, every last hearing, petitions ready, I'll speak for you, brother, as you no longer can.

*Don't say I don't hope.*

Don't let me open my desk drawer and let more fuckeries fly out.

Don't be a stranger anymore.

Don't ask me to hold my breath.

*Call me later tonight, okay?* Donna says before we even start our final descent, even though she herself is no stranger to death, her sister taken by pancreatic cancer a decade ago before the drugs and treatments they have now, Donna's positive, she's told me, positive her sister would have lived longer, more comfortably, like Jim, she says, and I bristle, can't help it, not the same thing, I think, but she's just trying to be kind, to share, she's my friend, maybe her sister's death and Jim's and Adrian's and my mom's and Dad's at a ripe ninety-three are the same thing in the end, an End, so I will call her, tonight and tomorrow and the day after next, we'll both adopt those dogs we've talked about, walk them in the park together, try agility training, treats and snuggles, I'll call mine Asa, fluffy and white, Bean for Donna's little dog, Listen to you! Jim would say, You softy, he'd tease.

*Back it up, buster, keep at it:* as if memories are an afterlife.

*A white planter on the windowsill,* tumble of leaves from a golden potus, a gift from a recent thesis advisee: requires little watering, say the instructions: perfect, given the state I'm in, always waiting for the knock on my door.

A time in-between, I believe that, I hope.

A chance to roll my chair closer to my desk and behold my face mirrored in the dark screen, hold my breath and in this way see: a student comes.

# ACKNOWLEDGEMENTS

While writing *Say This,* two phrases from writers whose work I admire accompanied me along the way. In *Eva Hurries Home,* the phrase "herself by herself," which Eva increasingly, defiantly feels she is becoming, is from Virginia Woolf's *To the Lighthouse.* In *Son One,* Lauryn's sense of some of her thought processes as evidence of her own "murder mind" borrows from Maggie Nelson's *The Red Parts.* I am grateful for the beacons of Woolf's and Nelson's works.

The ancient tradition of abecedarian writing informs *Son One.* Often found in religious Hebrew poems, as well as in a number of contemporary works, the form proceeds according to alphabetical order. Usually the first line or stanza begins with the first letter of the alphabet, and then moves on to each successive letter. In *Son One,* the first speaker's section—Lenore-May's—begins with an alphabetical sequence of 'a' words, followed by the next speaker—Jim's—whose section begins with 'b' words, and so on. I've used this form in first an ascending (a, b, c, d, e, etc.) and then a descending (z, y, x, w, etc.) pattern.

I'm deeply thankful for support from the heroic team at Biblioasis, especially Dan Wells and Vanessa Stauffer. Thank you also to Emily Donaldson and Natalie Olsen.

John Metcalf, without whom—seriously, I can't even begin to fully contemplate.

Thank you as well to Cynthia Holz, Michael Kimball, Vid Smooke for patiently reading drafts and providing insightful comments.

Thanks to Susie Brandt for the use of her glorious space, where I wrote some of this book.

Printed by Imprimerie Gauvin
Gatineau, Québec